DEEP, DARK SECRETS

Bess removed the manila envelope from her bag and pulled out a sheet of paper covered with scrawled handwriting: "Bess Marvin: This Is Your Life!"

She had a feeling she knew who'd written it, and when she read on, she was sure. "I've heard that you can tell a lot about a girl by the things she carries around with her."

"I don't believe this," Bess mumbled.

Brian leaned over her shoulder. He skimmed down the page, then burst out laughing. "Listen to this!" he said to Chris and Casey. " 'One date book, the mark of a truly intelligent and organized person. Obviously, you didn't buy it for yourself.' " Brian added, "Paul ought to know. He gave it to you, right?"

Bess was too embarrassed to answer. "Can we just get this over with?" she begged. Brian handed the sheet back to her, and Bess read the rest of it to herself.

"By now you might be wondering, What are Paul's deepest, darkest secrets? Tomorrow night could be your chance to find out. Say, at the movies? They're showing *Night Raiders* at the Cave at 7:30. Can you pencil me in?"

NANCY DREW ON CAMPUS™

Available from ARCHWAY Paperbacks

For orders other than by individual consumers, Pocket Books grants a discount on the purchase of **10 or more** copies of single titles for special markets or premium use. For further details, please write to the Vice-President of Special Markets, Pocket Books, 1633 Broadway, New York, NY 10019-6785 8th Floor.

For information on how individual consumers can place orders, please write to Mail Order Department, Simon & Schuster, Inc., 200 Old Tappan Road, Old Tappan, NJ 07675.

Nancy Drew on Campus™ #8

Getting Closer

Carolyn Keene

AN ARCHWAY PAPERBACK
Published by POCKET BOOKS
New York London Toronto Sydney Tokyo Singapore

The sale of this book without its cover is unauthorized. If you purchased this book without a cover, you should be aware that it was reported to the publisher as "unsold and destroyed." Neither the author nor the publisher has received payment for the sale of this "stripped book."

This book is a work of fiction. Names, characters, places and incidents are products of the author's imagination or are used fictitiously. Any resemblance to actual events or locales or persons, living or dead, is entirely coincidental.

AN ARCHWAY PAPERBACK *Original*

An Archway Paperback published by
POCKET BOOKS, a division of Simon & Schuster Inc.
1230 Avenue of the Americas, New York, NY 10020

Copyright © 1996 by Simon & Schuster Inc.
Produced by Mega-Books, Inc.

All rights reserved, including the right to reproduce
this book or portions thereof in any form whatsoever.
For information address Pocket Books, 1230 Avenue
of the Americas, New York, NY 10020

ISBN: 0-671-52754-1

First Archway Paperback printing April 1996

10 9 8 7 6 5 4 3 2 1

NANCY DREW, AN ARCHWAY PAPERBACK and colophon
are registered trademarks of Simon & Schuster Inc.

NANCY DREW ON CAMPUS is a trademark of
Simon & Schuster Inc.

Cover photos by Pat Hill Studio

Printed in the U.S.A.

IL 8+

Getting Closer

CHAPTER 1

Nancy Drew was glowing as she stood by the entrance of the Student Union. Every time she looked at the newspaper in her hands, a thrill swept through her from head to toe. She had been walking on air from the moment she'd picked up a copy of the paper that Wednesday afternoon.

Nancy couldn't stop staring at the three little words right below the headline of the article in the *Wilder Times:* "By Nancy Drew." Her name, in black and white. Right there on the front page.

"Feels good, doesn't it?" a deep voice spoke up next to Nancy.

"Jake!" she cried.

Before his name was even out of her mouth, Jake Collins was pulling her into a huge hug and deep kiss. His arms closed tightly around her, and Nancy melted against him, tingling from head to toe. She reached up automatically to touch his brown hair.

"To see your byline on the front page, I mean," Jake whispered. "Congratulations."

Nancy caught her breath, floating gently back down to earth. She leaned back just enough to look at her boyfriend.

She'd never known anyone like Jake before. With his thick hair and cowboy boots, he wasn't so much handsome as striking—and incredibly magnetic. The more she got to know him, the more she was drawn to him. Every time she looked into his eyes—irresistible rays of brown— she grew weak in the knees.

"So tell me, Ms. Drew," Jake said, holding an imaginary microphone in front of her as they headed indoors. "How does it feel to break the hottest story to hit Wilder this semester?"

Nancy felt a grin spread across her face. "Great. But you'd better watch what you say, Jake." She shot him a look of mock worry. "If you keep tossing out compliments like that, people will start to wonder what happened to the brutally honest, tough critic everyone on the paper is so intimidated by."

"I *am* being honest," Jake insisted. "That article was hot news *and* well written. That's my totally unbiased, objective opinion."

"Well, since you put it that way . . ." Nancy said slowly. She gazed intently into his eyes, drinking him in. "Then thanks."

The article was a major exposé about REACH,

a cultlike group that had recently been on campus and was led by a man who turned out to be more interested in his followers' money than their well-being.

Suddenly the sounds of shouting and laughter came from the back corner of the cavernous room they had entered.

"Par-ty . . . Par-ty . . . Par-ty!"

Nancy and Jake looked over to see a group of people squeezed around a table so that they blended into a fuzzy mass of arms, faces, clothes, and hair.

"Hey, Nancy, Jake!" Nancy's suitemate Reva Ross leaned away from the group and waved at Nancy. "Pull up a chair!"

"What's going on?" Nancy called over, laughing. "Did somebody win the lottery or something?" As she and Jake walked over to the table, Nancy saw that two more of her suitemates, Kara Verbeck and Liz Bader, were there, too.

"I wish," Reva's boyfriend, Andy Rodriguez, spoke up.

Kara grinned up at Nancy, her brown hair spilling over her shoulders. "Anyway, since when do we need an excuse to have a good time?"

"*You're* the one who had a reason to celebrate," Liz told Nancy. She nodded to the *Wilder Times* tucked under Nancy's arm. "I saw your article on REACH. Front page and everything. Congratulations!"

"Thanks," Nancy said simply, not wanting to

make a big deal about the article. The truth was, she was really proud of it, but talking about it made her feel self-conscious.

"I'm getting some fries," she said, changing the subject. "Anyone want anything?"

"I do. I'm starving," said Jake. "I'll come with you."

Half a dozen people also called out orders. While Nancy and Jake waited for the man at the grill to fill them, Nancy opened her copy of the *Times* again.

Nancy moved to the side as a man stepped past her, then she did a double take. It was Dan McCall, her journalism professor.

"Hello, Jake," Professor McCall said, nodding. He had a powerful build and blue eyes that seemed to pick out every detail.

When he saw Nancy, he tapped a copy of the *Wilder Times* that stuck out of the bulging briefcase tucked under his arm. "I read your article on REACH, Nancy. Nice job."

Nancy hadn't even realized that he knew who she was. Journalism 100 had dozens of people in it. There wasn't much opportunity for individual attention. "You liked it? Really?" she asked.

"It was organized, concise, interesting." Professor McCall ticked off the points on his fingers with the same straightforward style he used in class. "Keep up the good work." With another nod, he disappeared into the crowd.

"I told you I was being objective," Jake said.

Nancy felt a delicious shiver as he slipped an

arm around her waist and drew her close to him. "Why don't we go out to celebrate tonight?"

"Tonight?" Nancy blinked herself back to reality. "Well, I've got mountains of reading to do for—"

She didn't have a chance to finish her sentence, because Jake bent to cover her mouth in a long, sweet kiss that left her reeling. "I'll pick you up at eight," he murmured into her hair. "Okay?"

For a moment all Nancy could do was hang on to his flannel shirt. She felt so giddy, she was sure she'd fall if she let go of him. When she finally answered, her voice was a breathless whisper. "Sounds great."

"Watch your step, George." Will Blackfeather opened the door to the environmental science lab, then stepped back to let his girlfriend, George Fayne, angle through on her crutches.

"I can't wait until I get rid of these things, so I can walk around like a normal human being again," George said as she hobbled into the noisy corridor.

"You look all right to me," Will commented, his eyes sliding appreciatively over her lean curves. "Better than all right."

A second later she felt his lips on the back of her neck in a soft kiss. It was so electric that George stopped right in the middle of the hallway.

"If you're trying to make me forget that I have a sprained ankle," she breathed, "it's working."

"It's my own personal brand of medicine. Works every time," Will murmured. Straightening up, he shouldered her backpack over his own, his brown eyes sparkling. "Anytime you need help, just call on me."

"Gee, thanks." George laughed, blowing her dark brown curls off her forehead. "It's great to know that I'm going out with such a selfless, giving person."

"Absolutely," Will told her, keeping a straight face. "I want to do everything I can to help you recuperate. Let's say we schedule a session for"— he leaned forward and slipped an arm around her shoulders—"right now."

"I'd love to, but . . ." Reluctantly George pushed him away. "Shouldn't we be walking over to the Kaplan Arts Center? They're posting the final choice for the World of Art Show this afternoon, aren't they?"

Will took a deep breath and nodded. "At four o'clock," he answered, glancing at his watch. "I guess we should head that way. It's twenty of now."

"Not that I have any doubts about which show will be chosen," George said, as they made their way down the stairs to the exit. "Cherokee Traditions of Art, curated by Will Blackfeather."

Just talking about Will's show made her smile. It was hard to believe that less than a month had passed since Will had first told her that Wilder's Fine Arts Department was sponsoring a new series of art exhibits, called the World of Art. Each show would be organized by a student curator and chosen by jury committee. A week earlier they'd learned that the World of Art jury committee had narrowed the selection to three proposals, including Will's.

"I can't take all the credit," Will said, tweaking her nose. "You helped me write the proposal."

George groaned. "Only because I wound up with this bum ankle when I was training for the Earthworks race. You're the one who thought of exhibiting artifacts owned by the Cherokee in Oklahoma."

Will smiled at her—a wide, infectious grin that lit up his whole face. "It was partly just an excuse to get back in touch with people from the Cherokee Nation again," he said, shrugging. "My family kind of lost contact after we moved to South Dakota, back when I was in high school."

George shot him a sideways glance. "So, I guess the actual artifacts don't mean anything to you at all, huh?" she teased.

"Well, I wouldn't say *that*. . . ." Will said slowly. "Actually, Cherokee crafts are incredibly beautiful. You should see the weavings and pottery and ceremonial pipes and stuff. I mean, it's more than just art. Those things tell the story of my ancestors and our folklore."

George reached out and twined her fingers with Will's. "Sounds amazing," she told him.

"I wish I could be sure that the jury committee felt the same way we do." Will shrugged as he raked a hand through his straight black hair. "It seems like everyone's talking about Holly Thornton's proposal for Alternative Art and Design."

"Not everyone," George insisted. "Bess is in Holly's sorority, and she's rooting for your show to be chosen."

"Bess is your cousin," Will pointed out dryly. He leaned over to kiss her on the cheek. "But if you're trying to cheer me up, it's working."

"Glad to be of service," George said, grinning.

Will pushed open the main door to the science building, and a gust of cold wind hit George. "Anyway, people are only talking about Holly's show because they already know her and the artists she wants to exhibit," she said. "Face it. A lot of people don't know much about Native American art."

"Mmm," Will agreed. "I guess Frank Chung is in the same boat I am. I mean, Chinese art isn't exactly the hottest topic on campus, either."

Frank Chung was the third finalist, George recalled. He wanted to exhibit his family's private collection of Chinese art. "Well, I'm sure the jury's not going to be swayed by popular opinion. They'll judge all three proposals objectively," she said.

"I hope so," Will said.

"It's almost four. We'd better hurry." She threw him a teasing grin over her shoulder. "Come on. I'll race you."

Will's eyes lit up. "Sounds like a challenge. What does the winner get?" he asked.

George raised one eyebrow suggestively, then

shot forward on her crutches. "I'll tell you later. . . ."

"Study break!" Bess Marvin closed her bio notebook and flopped back against the couch in the living room of the Kappa sorority. "I don't know why anyone would actually choose to learn this stuff. Is there *any* way that knowing the reproductive system of the fruit fly is going to be important to me later in life?"

"Only if you're planning to marry one." Casey Fontaine grinned at Bess from the living room floor, where she sat surrounded by notecards.

Bess raised an eyebrow at Casey, shooting her a dubious glance. "I think you got out of L.A. just in time, Case," she said. "All those years in TV have totally warped you."

"That's why I went to L.A. in the first place, didn't you know? So I could turn into a social deviant," Casey shot back good-naturedly.

Bess shook her head, but she couldn't help laughing. Sometimes it was still hard to believe that she was friends with someone who had starred in a hit television series before beginning college. But that was Casey—a megastar. Tall and willowy, with short red hair and a face that was worshiped by guys across the country. At the beginning of the semester, Bess had thought that Casey might be just another spoiled Hollywood brat-packer. But that was before Casey moved into Nancy's suite. Before she and Bess acted together in *Grease!*, and before they both became

Kappa pledges. Now that Bess knew Casey, she had to admit that she was really great.

"Actually, I've got bugs on the brain," Casey admitted. "It's this paper I'm doing for comparative lit, on *The Metamorphosis*. It's about a guy who wakes up to find out he's turned into an insect."

"Yech. What a fate," Bess said, grimacing. "Did the poor guy have a girlfriend?"

Casey arched one of her russet brows. "Sounds like you've got a case of *romance* on the brain," she teased.

Bess smiled to herself, picturing Paul Cody's ruggedly handsome face. "Maybe," she admitted. "Too bad that so far most of the romance is only in my head."

"I've seen the way Paul Cody looks at you," Casey said knowingly. "And you are definitely *not* imagining things."

"I guess not," Bess said, her cheeks growing hot. "But between pledging Kappa, being in *Grease!*, and helping out with the Earthworks race, I've hardly have a chance to even talk to him."

Casey shot a look around the deserted living room. "Um, Bess? All that stuff has wound down, in case you hadn't noticed," she pointed out. "So shouldn't you be somewhere with Paul instead of hanging around here?"

"Actually, we have a sort-of date in a little while," Bess confided.

"A *sort-of* date?" Casey asked.

Bess pulled a small date book from beneath her bio notebook, opened it, and handed it to Casey.

" 'Ten minutes with Paul at Java Joe's,' " Casey read. "Bess, you can't even say hello in less than ten minutes. You'll never get to know the guy if this is all the time you're giving him."

"It was Paul's idea," Bess said, holding up her hands defensively. "He said that I was always so busy, he figured the only way to see me was to schedule himself in."

Casey stared at her, then broke out laughing. "Dating on the installment plan. Only you could come up with something so outrageous."

Bess opened her mouth to object, but Casey cut her off. "I know, I know. It was Paul's idea."

"The pathetic part is, I've been so tied up with other things that we've actually had to use these ten-minute slots in order to see each other," Bess said.

"And you think *I'm* warped?" Casey asked. "You've been sitting here for the last hour reading about fruit flies when you could have been with a guy who's obviously crazy about you."

"I needed to get some study time in," Bess insisted. "And that's been impossible in my dorm room lately."

"Leslie?" Casey guessed.

"You got it," Bess said with a groan. Her roommate, Leslie King, was premed, compulsively organized, and the complete opposite of Bess. "She's been pulling all-nighters at least twice a week. If I breathe too loudly, she practically bites my head off."

"Sounds painful," Casey joked, grimacing.

Bess laughed, but the truth was, she was starting to worry about Leslie. Leslie had always been a study-aholic, but the last few weeks she'd been even more stressed out than usual. Sometimes Bess slept on the couch at the sorority just to keep out of Leslie's way.

The sound of the sorority's front door opening and closing broke into Bess's thoughts. Soozie Beckerman appeared in the living room doorway, her straight blond hair brushed into a perfect geometric cut above her shoulders.

"Hi, Casey," Soozie said in a sugary voice. Then she saw Bess, and her smile faded. "Oh, hi," she added flatly.

"Hi," Bess said, but Soozie acted as if she wasn't even there. Sitting on one of the chairs, she started talking to Casey about some club in L.A. that Soozie had been to.

It never failed, Bess reflected. Whenever she was around, Soozie either just ignored her or said something really insulting. Bess knew it wasn't her fault. Soozie acted like that around *all* the pledges who were friends with Holly. But that didn't make it any easier to get used to.

Soozie broke off as the phone sounded from the kitchen. A moment later a voice called out, "Is Bess here?"

"Yes!" Bess jumped up from the couch, relieved to have an excuse to get away from Soozie.

She ran to the kitchen and grabbed the phone from a Kappa sister who was making a sandwich. " 'Lo?" Bess said into the receiver.

"Don't you *ever* spend time in your dorm anymore?" Brian Daglian's voice came over the line.

"Not if I can help it," she said, grinning. "What's up, Brian?"

She and Brian had both had a hard time adjusting to being in college. Getting to know him had saved her during the first few weeks of the semester. She'd even thought he might be boyfriend material—before he'd confided to her that he was gay. Now, he was her closest friend, besides Nancy and George.

"Don't tell me you forgot," Brian said.

Bess bit her lip and looked around the Kappas' kitchen, as if something there could tell her what he was talking about. "Well, um . . ."

"The Drama Club auditions," he reminded her. "Today's the last day to sign up."

"Oh, my gosh." Bess slapped herself on the forehead. "I am such an airhead!"

It had been days since Brian had told her about the Drama Club's next project, performing a series of one-act plays. "I was supposed to tell Casey, too," she went on, groaning. "I hope it's not too late."

"Call the Drama Department secretary right away to hold audition spots for you two," Brian said. "And this time, don't forget!"

"Thanks, Bri. You're a lifesaver," Bess told him. "I'll talk to you later, okay?"

She hung up the phone, then ran for the living room. "Casey, you're going to kill me!"

Casey and Soozie both turned to stare at her. "What happened?" Casey asked, looking worried.

There was no graceful way to say it, so Bess just blurted it out. "The Drama Club's holding auditions for a bunch of one-act plays, and today's the last day to sign up."

"You're kidding! I can't believe I didn't know about it," Casey said, jumping up from the couch. "I'm definitely signing up."

"Me, too, if I can keep my head screwed on to my body long enough to call the Drama Department," Bess said. "Sorry, Casey. I promised Brian I'd tell you, but I totally forgot until now."

"Don't worry about it," Casey said. She started for the kitchen, then stopped to look back at Bess. "Actually, you could be in bigger trouble than you thought, Bess," she said mysteriously.

"I could?" Bess started to worry—until she saw the teasing glint in Casey's green eyes.

"With Paul," Casey explained. "He's going to kill you when he finds out that you've got *another* extracurricular activity."

She picked up Bess's date book and tossed it to her. "You'd better not be late for your date," she added with a grin. "It might be the last chance you have to see him for a while."

"Voilà!" Eileen O'Connor announced. With a flourish she ripped off a large sketch she'd been working on and tacked it up on the studio wall. "What do you think?"

Holly Thornton stood back and looked critically at the charcoal drawing. For the last ten minutes Holly and B. J. Olson, a fine arts graduate student, had been in B.J.'s studio, posing for Eileen in front of B.J.'s latest sculpture—a mixed-media extravaganza of video screens, metal wire, old bolts, and neon lights.

"Great," she told Eileen. "You're really loosening up. And you've caught the essence of both figures."

"You think so?" Eileen asked, her freckled face lighting up with pleasure.

B.J. slid off the stool where he'd been sitting and came over to stand next to Holly. He pointed to the wild mop of hair that Eileen had drawn, then dug his fingers into his own wiry blond curls. "You've definitely caught the essence of a bad hair day," he said.

Turning to Holly, he added, "Hey, maybe you should put *this* piece into the World of Art exhibit."

At the mention of the exhibit, Holly buzzed with excitement. It would be a major boost to her career to curate the premiere show of the World of Art series. But she had to remind herself that it wasn't a done deal yet.

"We don't know which proposal the jury committee's chosen," she told B.J. and Eileen. "They won't post their decision for"—she shot a quick look at her watch—"five more minutes."

"Everyone I've talked to said the committee would be crazy not to go with your proposal," Eileen spoke up. "An exhibit of alternative art and design by Wilder students."

"Including a piece by artistic genius Bjorn J. Olson," B.J. put in. He stepped forward to tap a video screen that was built into his sculpture, with copper wire wrapped artfully around it.

Holly couldn't hold back the grin that spread across her face. She felt good about her proposal. The work she'd chosen was very strong. And it *did* make sense to start the series with a show by the university's own students.

"A lot could hinge on this for me," she confided. "Double Negative Design is looking for a summer intern. Their personnel director told me that if I got this show, that would pretty much guarantee me the spot."

"I'm impressed. Double Negative Design does the window designs for the most innovative stores in the country," Eileen said, her hazel eyes widening.

"Not to mention that a summer job could lead to something permanent after graduation," B.J. added.

Holly had already thought about that—over and over. "Well," she said, looking back and forth between B.J. and Eileen. "It's zero hour. Will you guys come with me?"

"Try to stop us," Eileen said.

The three of them made their way through the paint-splattered studios and down to the third floor of Kaplan. The department offices were located along a balcony that overlooked the main gallery, on the second floor. As Holly, B.J., and Eileen came out of the stairwell, Holly saw Will and George coming from the escalator. They arrived at the offices just as a secretary pinned up a sheet of paper on the bulletin board there.

Holly stopped a few feet away, her palms sweaty. Get a hold of yourself, she ordered, shaking herself. She made herself take the last few steps and look at the announcement: Wilder University's Fine Arts Department is pleased to announce . . .

"Blah, blah, blah," Holly murmured. Her eyes flew impatiently to the end of the short paragraph, looking for the name of the show that had been chosen.

When she saw the words, Holly's eyes widened in surprise. "No way! I can't believe this!"

CHAPTER 2

Will vaguely thought he heard Holly saying something, but everything was a blur except for the words he was reading: "Cherokee Traditions of Art. Student Curator: Will Blackfeather." He had to read it five times before it sank in. "We did it!" he shouted.

"Fantastic!" George flung her arms around him, and Will caught her up and swung her around. When he put her down again, she was grinning from ear to ear.

Will was so psyched, he couldn't stand still. "I feel like someone just pumped about a gallon of adrenaline into my bloodstream," he said, giving George's shoulders a squeeze. "Wow, unbelievable! I mean, I really never thought ..."

"*I* did," George whispered, her brown eyes filled with emotion. "I knew you could do it."

"*We,*" he insisted, moving his mouth toward hers. "We're a team, remember?"

18

"Mmm."

She leaned closer, pressing her lips against his, and one simple word flitted through Will's mind. Perfect, he thought. Everything is absolutely—

"Excuse me," an annoyed voice spoke up from behind them.

Will let out a sigh and pulled away from George. He caught sight of short black hair and the preppy, button-down shirt of a guy who pushed past him and George to look at the bulletin board. When the guy turned around, he frowned at Will and George.

"I guess it doesn't take a genius to figure out that you're Will Blackfeather," he said.

Will exchanged an uncomfortable glance with George. "That's—"

Before he could even get out the *me,* the guy stepped back toward the escalator. "Congrats," he said flatly. Then he was gone.

"What's *his* problem?" George muttered, staring after the guy.

"That was Frank Chung, the other finalist," Holly Thornton spoke up. "Don't take it personally. He's probably just disappointed."

Will had been so focused on the announcement that he hadn't really noticed Holly. Now he saw that she was with Eileen and a tall guy he didn't recognize. Stepping away from them, Holly came over to Will and held out her hand. "Congratulations, Will. Hi, George."

"Yeah, congratulations," Eileen added.

Both girls smiled, but Will could read the dis-

19

appointment on their faces. "Thanks," he said uncertainly.

"Well, see you around." Brushing her honey blond hair over shoulder, Holly turned to Eileen and the guy they were with. The three of them were whispering as they walked away. Will caught the looks they threw him before they disappeared into the stairwell.

"Is it my imagination, or did the temperature just drop in here?" Will said in a low voice. "Something tells me they think the jury committee made a mistake."

"Not your problem," George said. "I mean, I feel bad for Holly, but the committee definitely made the right choice."

Will couldn't help smiling. "I can't wait to tell Dan," he said, thinking out loud. "He'll be unbelievably psyched."

"Dan?" George echoed, raising an eyebrow. "He's the man who runs the museum back in Oklahoma?"

Will nodded. "Dan Chekelelee. He worked with a gallery owner from Tulsa named Seth Klein to choose the pieces that'll be in the show. Seth isn't Cherokee, but he specializes in Cherokee art. Dan's too busy to leave Oklahoma right now, so Seth agreed to oversee the installation at the gallery here."

George shot him a teasing glance. "You two are going to be working overtime to get the show up in time. It's supposed to open in just a few weeks, isn't it?"

"It's a little overwhelming, but I worked out a schedule with Dan," Will said. "His men are going to pack the most valuable artifacts right away, so that Seth Klein can bring them with him on the first available plane. That could be as soon as tomorrow morning. While Seth and I figure out the layout of the show, Dan will pack the rest of the artifacts and ship them within a few days."

Will brushed his fingers up and down George's arm as he thought through the rest of the details. "The museum here has pedestals and everything else we'll need to mount the show," he went on. "And Dan's already worked out a design for the announcement. He's sending it up with Seth Klein. If I like it, there's a place in town that can have them printed up by Monday."

"I'm impressed," George told him. "Sounds like you've taken care of all the details. Except one."

"What's that?" Will asked, searching his mind. There *were* a lot of details. . . .

"Figuring out how *I* can help," George answered.

Will let his eyes sweep over her face. "Don't worry about that," he murmured. "I'll think of something."

Bess pulled open the door to Java Joe's and ran inside. Her eyes swept over the faces packed into the coffee bar. It took only a second to find Paul in a flannel shirt and jeans, sitting at a table next to the front window. He looked so cute, she couldn't believe every other girl in the coffee bar wasn't falling all over him.

When Paul saw her, a playful smile spread across his face. "Seven minutes left, and counting down," he said, pointing to his wristwatch. "By the time you get some coffee, our date will be officially over."

"Sorry. I got held up at the sorority," Bess said. "Maybe we can stretch it out a little, unofficially." She slid into the seat opposite him and threw the strap of her bag over the back of her chair.

"Don't tell me we might be able to have an actual conversation," Paul said, feigning disbelief.

"It's been known to happen once or twice before," Bess shot back with a grin.

Paul fixed her with an intense look that sent a delicious shiver through her. "All I care about is that it keeps *on* happening."

Looking into his blue eyes, she could hardly believe she'd almost passed on the chance to get to know him. From now on, she promised herself, I'm going to make time for Paul, no matter how crazy my life gets.

Paul softly stroked her cheek and said, "Let's just keep making these little appointments together, okay?"

Bess jumped up abruptly. "Appointments? Oh, my gosh," she breathed. "How could I forget— again!"

"Huh?" Paul looked up at her. "What are you talking about, Bess?"

Grabbing her shoulder bag, she plunked it down on the table and began dumping things out, looking for her change purse. "I need to call the Drama Department, pronto. Auditions," she explained. "If I don't get one, I'll—"

She broke off, grabbing the small leather pouch from her purse. "Aha!" She jumped up and started for the pay phones at the rear of the coffee bar, but something made her stop.

Turning back to Paul, she saw that he was staring numbly at the jumbled mess that had spilled from her bag. "I must be crazy," she heard him mumble to himself.

"Sorry, Paul," she called back to him. "I'll make it up to you, I promise."

He looked at her, his eyes gleaming with anticipation. "That's one promise I'm going to make sure you keep."

Ginny Yuen sat cross-legged in the threadbare armchair in Ray Johannson's dorm room. The rest of the room was filled with equipment—a couple of electric guitars, drums, some amplifiers. Even Ray's desk, which held the only signs of college—books and class papers—had stacks of music CDs on it. The whole place was all about music, just like Ray.

Ray sat on his bed facing Ginny. Bent over his acoustic guitar, he strummed out the chords of a song they'd been working on. As he played, a look of gentle concentration was etched into his face. Ginny loved his face when it got that look.

Ray stopped strumming long enough to glance up at her. "What do you think of it?" he asked.

"I love it," she said truthfully. "The tune is really—"

"I meant the goatee," Ray corrected. Smiling at her, he brushed his fingers through the tuft of dark hair on his chin. "You haven't said anything since I started growing it."

Actually, Ginny wasn't sure what she thought of his goatee. It hid the amazingly strong lines of his chin and she still wasn't used to the tickling sensation whenever they kissed. Still, she didn't want to get on his case about it.

"It's really distinctive," she told him, trying to sound upbeat. "Makes you look older."

"Distinctive, huh?" Ray gave her a bemused look, then went back to strumming.

Lyrics, Ginny reminded herself. You're supposed to be writing lyrics.

She shot a rueful glance at the sea of crumpled-up, scribbled-on sheets of paper that littered the floor. Just let the music wash over you, she ordered herself. The right words will come.

Ginny leaned back and closed her eyes. The chords were mysterious, compelling. They made her feel as if she were in an unknown place that was beautiful and romantic and just a little bit scary.

"Close your eyes and ride the magic.
  Forget the past. We're falling fast.
  Open up your heart and jump into the void."

When she opened her eyes, Ray was looking at her with shining eyes. "What are you saying, that being with me is like jumping off a cliff without a parachute?" he teased.

Ginny could feel her cheeks redden. "Something like that," she admitted. "What do you think? Will it work in the song?"

"Definitely." Ray pulled over the sheet music that lay on the table next to him and made a few adjustments to the notes dotted across the page. "Okay, here goes," he said under his breath. He strummed the new chords, humming the tune, while she filled in the words.

As the last chord faded to silence, Ray looked up at Ginny with a grin that lit up his whole face. "Sounds good. Let's call it 'Freefall,'" he said. "Maybe we can finish it in time to play with the other tunes on the air next week."

"On the air," Ginny echoed, grinning back at him. "I can't believe it. In just seven days the Beat Poets are going to play live on the campus radio station. I guess making that demo tape really helped you guys get a bigger audience."

Ray's band had been playing gigs on campus since the beginning of the semester. They'd gotten a lot of local press—so much that a local recording studio had offered them free studio time to record a demo tape. They'd just finished the tape the week before and had sent copies to some recording companies and all the local radio stations. Within days a DJ at KWUR had called to invite them to play on the air. Every time

Ginny thought about it, a shiver of excitement shot through her.

"I feel like such a celebrity. It's so . . ." She leaned back against the chair and drew up her legs, smiling.

"What?" Ray asked. He leaned forward and brushed a lock of hair from her eyes.

Ginny tried to put her thoughts into words. "It's so, amazing. I mean, six months ago I didn't even know what a demo tape was. I always had a plan, you know. Studying, medical school, my own practice. If anyone had told me that I'd be writing songs . . ."

"Dating a degenerate rock-and-roller like me," Ray put in, twanging a few exaggerated chords on his guitar.

"Falling in love with the most incredible musician I've ever met," she said, touching his hand. "You've changed everything for me, Ray."

And my own family doesn't know anything about you, a small voice in the back of her mind spoke up.

It wasn't that she didn't want to tell her parents. She did. But they were so "Old World" and strict, and Ray was . . . well, Ray. Ginny had a feeling that her mom and dad just wouldn't understand what an unbelievably special person he was. They'd take one look at his tattoo and earring and totally hate him.

"You look so serious," Ray said softly, breaking into her thoughts. "What's on your mind?"

Ginny shook herself, smiled at him. "Nothing,"

she said. "I just never knew life could be like this, that's all."

"It can be better," he said in the rich, gravelly voice that made him such a sexy singer. Ray put his guitar down and leaned toward her, playing his lips softly over her cheeks.

Ginny closed her eyes. Next week, she promised herself. I'll tell Mom and Dad about Ray next week.

"What do you think?" Jake asked Nancy that night. "Are you glad we came here?"

Nancy looked around Eritrea, the exotic Ethiopian restaurant where Jake had brought her to celebrate the publication of her article on REACH. The tables were low to the ground and set into scalloped alcoves. Instead of chairs, they sat on a thick carpet and leaned against large silk pillows that were propped against the walls. It was so intimate, luxurious, and romantic—more like lounging than eating.

"It's perfect," she said truthfully.

As Jake shifted against the pillows, his leg pressed against her knee, sending a ripple of pleasure through her.

"There's a little more spiced beef," he said. "You have it."

He broke off a piece of bread and used it to scoop up the last dollop of meat and sauce. He popped it into her mouth, then licked a speck from his fingers.

"I don't know how you do it," she said, shaking herself. "You bring me to a place that doesn't have chairs, or even silverware, and make it such a romantic adventure."

"Less is more," Jake said, grinning.

"That's just what I was thinking," she murmured.

A shadow fell across the table, and their waiter appeared, wearing a flowing red robe. "Would you like some coffee or dessert?" he asked.

"No, thanks," Jake answered, his brown eyes locking on Nancy. "We've got other plans for after dinner."

Nancy's heart skipped a beat. "We do?"

Jake nodded. "You'll see," he said mysteriously.

She practically floated outside to Jake's car. Things were so right between them, so natural. She didn't even feel the need to say anything. As Jake pulled out of the parking lot, she leaned back and let her mind wander.

During dinner, she and Jake had hardly spoken about the newspaper or their classes. But now Nancy found herself thinking about Dan McCall and the latest assignment he'd given her journalism class.

Objective reporting. They had to do a profile of a campus organization without making any value judgments. It didn't sound too hard, but Professor McCall had warned that keeping an objective distance wasn't always so easy.

Nancy had already chosen an organization

from the list McCall had handed out. All she had to do now was call to arrange an interview.

"Call *who* for an interview?"

Nancy's eyes popped open, and she saw Jake's gaze shift briefly to her. She didn't even realize she'd spoken out loud. "I was just thinking about my assignment for journalism," she said. "I'm going to interview Max Krauser, the guy who runs Helping Hands."

"That's kind of like a big brother program, isn't it?" Jake asked.

"And big sisters," she teased. "It's for kids from single-parent homes who don't have brothers or sisters of their own. Wilder students try to fill the role, spend time with them, listen to what they have to say."

"Great," Jake said. "Actually, Helping Hands gets pretty good press on campus. They help out with a big casino weekend the fraternities put on every year to raise money for charity—the Black and White Nights."

"I guess I'll hear about that during my interview," Nancy said with a shrug. "I have to be objective in my article, but I'm thinking of becoming a big sister myself after it's written."

"Great idea. Especially if you can adopt an overgrown journalism major who's desperately in need of TLC?"

"Well . . ." She pretended to think about it. "You do act like a high school kid sometimes."

Jake flicked his eyes away from the windshield just long enough to grin at her. "I object to that."

"Actually, I was thinking more along the lines of a little *sister*," Nancy finished.

"So, you're passing me over for another girl." Jake let out an exaggerated sigh. "In that case ..." He pulled the car to a stop and turned to her. "I think there's a high school girl out there who's going to be very lucky," he said.

"Good answer," she murmured. Glancing out the window, she saw that he'd parked on a small rise in the middle of nowhere. As far as the eye could see there was nothing but bare farmland and gently rolling hills. Above, the night sky was carpeted with stars. "I thought we were going somewhere for dessert," she said breathlessly.

Jake leaned in, covered her mouth in a steamy, passionate kiss. "We are," he whispered, his lips hovering just over hers. "Any objections to the menu?"

As he slid his arms around her, Nancy wished that he'd hold her this way forever. "No," she whispered back. "None at all."

CHAPTER 3

Uh-oh. She's humming." George's voice came from the doorway to Nancy's room Thursday morning. "It's not even nine o'clock yet, and she's humming."

Nancy stopped brushing her hair and turned to see George and Bess standing in the open doorway, grinning at her.

"I see roses," Bess added, nodding at the two deep red flowers that were stuck in a soda bottle on Nancy's dresser. "All right, Nancy, time to come down off that cloud, face the world of classes, tests . . ." she joked.

"Come on in, you guys," Nancy said, laughing. She nodded at Kara's empty bed. "Kara already left for breakfast."

George shook her head in amazement as she came in and sat down on Kara's bed. "Well, I guess we don't need to ask how last night's date was," she said. "I'd say you reached nirvana."

"Pretty close," Nancy admitted. "Things between Jake and me are really great."

"As if we couldn't guess," Bess put in slyly.

Just thinking about the night before made Nancy feel a glow all over. "He's so unbelievably . . ."

"Sexy? Smart?" George supplied.

"Romantic? Gorgeous?" Bess suggested.

Nancy grinned. "All of the above."

She could feel herself getting embarrassed, so she grabbed an envelope from her desk and tucked it into her backpack along with her books. "I'm starved. Let's go eat."

"Writing home?" Bess guessed.

Nancy nodded. "I'm sending Dad and Hannah a copy of my article."

She knew that her dad was keeping a scrapbook of all the things she sent home—articles, programs from concerts and plays, anything she sent him—but Nancy knew that they couldn't really know what her life was like at Wilder.

Not until they met Jake Collins. But the way things were going, she knew it would be time for him to meet them soon.

Jake cradled a cup of coffee in his hands and looked blearily down at the textbook that lay open on the table. He'd been trying to catch up on his reading, but it wasn't easy. Every time he looked down at the page, he kept thinking about Nancy Drew instead of the words.

"So, when are we going to meet her?" a voice spoke up.

Jake groaned as the image of Nancy vaporized and the print of his textbook stared back at him again. Nick Dimartini, one of his roommates, came into the kitchen of their second-floor apartment.

"Couldn't you knock or something?" Jake asked. "You just wrecked a perfectly good daydream."

Nick raked a hand through his uncombed, short, dark hair and reached for a coffee mug. "What are you saying? That you were out last night until one in the morning with a figment of your imagination?"

"Only a psych major would analyze his own roommate this early in the morning," Jake mumbled, shaking his head.

"And only a journalist would twist the facts around to keep from answering a direct question," Nick shot back.

"So when *are* we going to meet this Nancy Drew?"

This time it was Dennis Larkin, Jake's other roommate, talking. The tall junior came into the kitchen from the living room, shifting his books from hand to hand as he pulled on a leather jacket that was the same chocolate brown as his skin.

Jake gave up on his reading and flipped the book shut. "You'll meet her when you meet her."

Dennis shot Jake a dubious glance. "If you say so. Sure you're not hiding her from us?"

"Afraid of the competition?" Nick asked.

Jake didn't even bother commenting on that one.

"Or that we'll tell her what a lunatic the *real* Jake Collins is?" Dennis added.

"I'm quaking with fear," Jake deadpanned.

He was confident that what he and Nancy had was solid. So solid that it was almost scary.

"Get ready," George's roommate, Pam Miller, said as the two of them stepped into the cavernous room that housed Wilder's Nautilus equipment. "This is going to be the meanest, hardest workout of your life."

"Sounds like fun," George said doubtfully. She looked over the room—full of gleaming machines and sweaty students grunting as they strained against weights. "The doctor said I should do some *light* workouts. I don't need to . . ."

Just then a tall guy wearing shorts and no shirt walked past. His blond hair was damp with perspiration. Every time he moved, muscles rippled across his gleaming torso.

"Wow," George murmured. "I think I just discovered the best spectator sport at Wilder."

"Not that you're interested, right?" Pam laughed. "You have a boyfriend, remember?"

"Oh. Yeah. Right." George shook herself and grinned at her roommate.

Looking at the weight machines, she said, "I guess it can't hurt to work out a *little*," she said. "Especially if I want to have any chance of making the track team."

Pam readjusted her headband, scanning the room. "There's Kate and Eileen," she announced, pointing to a bench-press machine in the middle of the room.

George spotted Kate Terrell's reddish brown hair and wide, freckled face. She was wearing a workout leotard and tights with a sleeveless T-shirt over them. Eileen O'Connor was lying on her back on the padded bench, wearing running shorts and a baggy T-shirt.

"You two are just in time," Eileen said when she saw George and Pam. She let the weights clatter down and sat up, her face red and sweaty. Lowering her voice, she gestured to the left with her eyes. "Cute-butt alert."

George followed Eileen's gaze. Three guys were working out in T-shirts and nylon shorts that looked as if they were glued to their bodies.

"Talk about gorgeous," Kate murmured.

"Can we help you girls with something?" one of the guys called over.

George felt her face turn bright red. All three guys were grinning at them. They'd been caught blatantly checking the guys out!

"We'll be glad to show you how to use the machines," one of the other two added.

"I'll bet," Kate said, laughing.

"What do you say, George?" Pam added, shooting her a teasing glance. "Do you need a little *extra* coaching?"

George shook her head. "You guys are hopeless," she muttered to Kate, Pam, and Eileen. Then she called over to the guys, "We can handle ourselves."

"Suit yourselves," said the third guy. With a shrug he turned away from them.

When George turned around, she saw that Pam, Kate, and Eileen were all staring at her as if she'd lost her mind.

"We *are* supposed to be working out, aren't we?" she reminded them. "Anyway"—she lowered her voice a notch—"we can still look."

"Definitely," Eileen agreed. Grinning, she got up from the machine she'd been using and patted the bench. "Your horse awaits, George."

Taking a deep breath, George lay back on the bench and slowly started pumping weights with her arms. After just a minute she let go and sat up.

"I'm a total marshmallow," she groaned.

"Take it slow," Pam advised.

"Try something else," Kate suggested. She bent down and picked up some free weights that rested on the floor next to the Nautilus machine. "Eileen and I were afraid the machines might be too intense, so we picked up these, too."

While George pumped the weights with her arms, Pam gently rotated George's wounded ankle. "How's that?" she asked George. "Does it hurt?"

"It feels tight but good," George decided.

"If you're lucky, maybe you'll be off your crutches by the time the World of Art show opens," Eileen said hopefully. "You and Will must be really psyched."

"We are," George said.

She felt a little uneasy talking about the show with Eileen. She knew Eileen and Holly were friends. And it had been obvious the day before that they were disappointed that Holly's show wasn't chosen. On the other hand, Eileen *had* brought it up.

"I know that you and Holly are sorority sisters and art majors and everything," George said. "I just hope there's no bad feelings about Will's show being picked."

"Don't worry about it. I'm not about to hold a grudge," Eileen said, with an easy smile. "And neither is Holly."

George breathed a sigh of relief. "It's good to hear that," she admitted. "I wasn't sure. I mean, Holly seemed pretty unhappy yesterday."

Eileen shrugged. "Getting the show was important to her. She had a summer job that practically hinged on it, at Double Negative Design. Now it looks like she won't get it. But that's life, I guess."

Eileen's right, George thought as she went back to lifting her free weights. It's not that big a deal, and Holly's a decent person. She'll get over it.

Will stood in front of the entrance to the Kaplan Center for the Arts on Thursday afternoon. For the last half hour he'd kept his eyes glued to the road that curved up to the building from the university's main drive. He expected Seth Klein to be pulling up any minute, in a van carrying rare artifacts from the Cherokee Nation.

Will frowned as the chimes in the ivy-covered clock tower rang out four o'clock. Dan Chekelelee had told him that Seth's plane was due to land in Chicago before one. The airport was only an hour's drive from Wilder. Even if it took Seth a while to get his rental van and load the artifacts into it, he should have been here by now.

Will was just wondering if he should check on the flight, when he caught sight of a bright yellow rental van snaking along the main drive. The man in the front seat had a cellular phone stuck to his ear. As he turned onto the road leading to the arts center, he looked around tentatively, as if he wasn't sure he was in the right place.

"Bingo," Will murmured.

Seconds later the van pulled to a stop in front of the row of double doors that made up the entrance to Kaplan. Will jogged toward the van, feeling more pumped up every second. "Hi," he said, as the driver's door opened. "Are you Seth Klein?"

The man who stepped out of the van looked

as if he was in his early thirties, with tanned skin and a carefully brushed mane of sandy brown hair. He wasn't as tall or muscular as Will, and his look was slickly casual—jeans, snakeskin boots, shearling jacket. He was so busy talking into his cellular phone that he didn't seem to have seen or heard Will.

"Don't panic, Kelly," he was saying. "Just call back Oklahoma City and remind them that we're on a tight schedule. We can't wait until—"

The man broke off as his gray eyes focused on Will. "I have to go," he said into the phone. "I'll check in later.... Yeah. Okay, 'bye." Then he folded up the phone and stuck it into the pocket of his jacket. "Will Blackfeather?" he asked, smiling.

Will nodded and held out his hand. "You must be Seth Klein."

"The one and only," Seth answered easily. "Man, am I glad to see you. It took me forever to get this rental, and then I got lost on the drive from the airport." While he spoke, he walked to the back of the van, unlocked the rear door, and opened it. "We've got seven boxes. Let's get them unloaded, okay? I've got a lot of other business to take care of."

Seth seemed nice, in a frantic sort of way. He definitely appeared to have a lot going on. "Other business?" Will echoed.

Seth nodded. "We're putting up a show in my gallery in Tulsa. Half a dozen of the pieces are late arriving, one needs to be repaired." Seth shook his head good-naturedly. "Total mayhem. My assistant is freaking out."

"Sounds like you've got your hands full," Will said. "Come on. I'll help you unload this stuff. The storage room is right next to the gallery. It's got a security camera that'll be on around the clock. There are two keys, one for each of us."

"Sounds good," Seth said, nodding.

Taking one cardboard box, Will led the way through the entrance to an open foyer with a cathedral ceiling that rose three stories high. Escalators went up to the gallery space on the second floor and administrative offices on the third.

"Nice," Seth said approvingly when Will got off the escalator at the second-floor gallery. "I'd love to have a place this big. Not that I could afford it. It's a pretty rough time for the art market. My gallery's barely breaking even."

This guy sure does like to talk about himself, Will thought, smiling to himself. So far, he hadn't said a word about the Cherokee artifacts.

"Dan tells me you've done a lot of work with the people of the Cherokee Nation," Will said. He headed for an alcove at the rear of the gallery that connected to a back hallway and offices. That was where the storeroom was.

"Yeah. Dan and I met when he was raising money for his museum. I know a little about Cherokee art, and I guess he appreciated that. We've helped each other out ever since. I show contemporary work of Cherokee artists, and he lets me collaborate on some of the shows he puts up in his museum."

"Sounds good," Will said.

Seth nodded. "You're going to be bowled over when you see the artifacts I brought," he went on. "Talk about valuable. I'd give about anything to get the commission on just one or two of those pieces."

"They're not for sale, are they?" Will asked, shooting Seth a surprised glance. "I mean, Dan wouldn't—"

"He'd never even consider it," Seth said with a rueful smile. "Unfortunately for me."

Will looked at him warily—until he realized that Seth was just joking. Shaking his head, Will unlocked the storeroom door and flicked on the light. "Let's put these down and get the rest of the boxes up here," Will said. "I know you've got a lot of other business to take care of."

CHAPTER 4

Let me get this straight." Bess flipped through the sheaf of photocopied pages that Professor Farber had handed out. It was Thursday afternoon, and she, Brian, Casey, and Chris Vogel were sitting at the back of the room where the Drama Club had just finished meeting. "We have to learn *all* of these lines *and* be ready for auditions by the middle of next week?"

Brian leaned back in his chair and started to sing "The Impossible Dream."

"These are one-act plays, not a musical," Casey interrupted, tapping him on the crown of his head. "Think you can stay serious long enough to do drama?"

"My life *is* drama," Brian insisted.

Bess didn't miss the look that he and Chris exchanged. She was one of the few people who knew that Brian was gay—much less that he and

42

Chris were interested in each other. Even though Brian had told his parents, he and Chris kept a very low profile on campus.

"I don't know about you guys," Bess said, "but I'm going to have to rehearse nonstop. Even then I probably don't stand a chance of getting a part."

Casey rolled her eyes at Bess. "Will someone please strangle her?" she said. "You'll do great, Bess. But if you want, we could practice our lines together. It definitely helps to work with someone else."

"You'd do that for me?" Bess asked.

"Actually, I'd be doing it for *me*," Casey explained. "I'm more used to comedy than straight drama. I could use some pointers myself."

"Well, since you put it that way."

Bess bent to pick up her shoulder bag from the floor, then paused when she saw the large manila envelope inside. She'd found it outside her door but hadn't had time to open it yet. Now that the meeting was over, she pulled the envelope out and slid her finger under the flap to loosen it.

She pulled out a single sheet of paper that was covered with scrawled handwriting: "Bess Marvin: This Is Your Life!"

She had a feeling she knew who'd written it, and when she read on, she was sure. " 'I've heard that you can tell a lot about a girl by the things she carries around with her. Since you dumped the contents of your bag right under my nose in

43

Java Joe's, I decided to put that theory to the test.' "

"I don't believe this," Bess mumbled, grinning.

Brian leaned over her shoulder. He skimmed down the page, then burst out laughing. "Listen to this!" he said to Chris and Casey.

He plucked the paper from Bess's hands and read the first paragraph aloud. Then he began reciting the list Paul had made of the contents of Bess's purse: " 'Here's what I found,' " Brian read. " 'Nine assorted pens, pencils, and markers. I'd say you can never find a single one when you need it.' "

Casey and Chris both burst out laughing.

" 'Two notes to yourself,' " Brian read on. " 'Register for classes" and "Call Casey about auditions." Either you're getting a serious jump-start on next year, or you need to clean out your bag more often.' "

"It's true," Bess moaned. "I'm hopelessly disorganized."

Brian shot her a look of mock disbelief. "Who, *you?*" he said, before turning back to the list. " 'One article on REACH, written by Nancy Drew. You are a devoted friend.' "

Casey grinned up at Bess and said, "I'd have to agree with that one."

"Anything else?" Chris wanted to know.

Brian nodded. " 'One date book,' " he read. " 'The mark of a truly intelligent and organized person. Obviously, you didn't buy it for yourself.' " Brian raised an eyebrow and added, "Paul ought to know. He gave it to you, right?"

Bess was too embarrassed to answer. "Can we just get this over with?" she begged.

"Here's the last item," Brian told her. " 'One lipstick: Passionfruit. I'll tell you in person what I think of that.' "

Brian and Chris both whistled.

"What a lunatic," Bess mumbled, burying her face in her hands.

"I'd say he shows amazing insight," Brian teased. He handed the sheet back to her, and Bess read the rest of it to herself:

"By now you might be wondering, What are Paul's deepest, darkest secrets? Tomorrow night could be your chance to find out. Say, at the movies? They're showing *Night Raiders* at the Cave at 7:30. Can you pencil me in?"

The note was signed simply *P*.

Bess smiled to herself as she put the sheet down and pulled her date book from her shoulder bag. Opening it up to Friday, she wrote in "Paul" in big letters.

"Thanks a lot for talking to me, Max. Helping Hands sounds great," Nancy told Max Krauser, the senior who ran the organization.

Max stood up behind the desk where he'd been sitting, in the cramped, windowless room where Helping Hands had its office. "Hey, I'm glad of the free publicity," he said, shaking her hand.

Nancy had to resist the urge to tell him right

then and there that she was planning to sign up to be big sister herself. This was supposed to be objective reporting, after all.

Max Krauser wasn't at all what she'd expected. She'd been sure he would be tall and muscular—a larger-than-life superhero type. Instead, he wasn't very tall *or* particularly muscular. But he had an irresistible enthusiasm. After talking with him, Nancy was convinced that he was the main reason Helping Hands was so successful.

As she headed out into the late afternoon, Nancy glanced at the clock tower. Four-thirty. She might as well head over to the newspaper office and start writing up the interview.

And find Jake.

All day long, at the oddest times, her thoughts had kept jumping to him. In the middle of classes. While she was at the salad bar at the cafeteria. It was about time she got a dose of the real thing.

When she stepped into the newspaper office ten minutes later, her head turned automatically to the messy corner desk that was Jake's home away from home.

It was empty.

Stifling her disappointment, Nancy sat down in front of one of the terminals and flicked it on. As the computer whirred and beeped into action, she took out her notes from the interview and spread them out.

But somehow, she just couldn't concentrate on them. Ever since her date with Jake the night before, she was having a hard time concentrating on anything except what it felt like to be in his arms.

Get a grip! Nancy ordered, shaking herself. You've got work to do!

She pulled her mini-recorder from her bag and hit the rewind button.

Maybe he's at his apartment, a small voice at the back of her mind spoke up. Sure, we both have things to do, but we could get some work done while we're together.

Nancy turned her computer off again and started shoving her notebook and recorder back in her bag.

"Finished already?" a voice spoke up from across the room.

Looking that way, Nancy saw Gail Gardeski, the paper's editor-in-chief. Gail was sitting in front of the usual mountain of papers on her desk. There was a smudge of newsprint on her long, thin nose, and her serious eyes were focused on Nancy.

"Writer's block," Nancy hedged.

Usually, she tried to play down her relationship with Jake whenever she was here. She didn't want Gail or anyone else to think that she expected special treatment just because she was dating the paper's top reporter.

"In that case, could you give me a hand?" Gail asked. "I'm not sure I like the layout of the editorial page. Would you mind taking a look and telling me what you think?"

For just a moment Nancy considered making

an excuse so she could leave and find Jake. But it wasn't every day that Gail Gardeski asked her opinion about an editorial layout. This was really a great opportunity. She couldn't just blow it off, even if she did want to be with Jake.

Nancy put a smile on her face. "Sure," she answered. "I'd love to."

"Ouch," George said to herself as she pulled open the heavy double doors to the Kaplan Center for the Arts.

As soon as she was inside, she stopped and rubbed the aching muscles of her upper arms. "Sorry, guys," she murmured. "I know you'd be a lot happier if I were in the sauna right now."

Kate, Pam, and Eileen were still at the sports complex, soaking up the dry heat of the sauna after their workout. But George had decided to skip the sweatbox and come here instead.

She and Will hadn't made a plan to meet, but she hoped he wouldn't mind her showing up out of the blue. He'd already invited her, Bess, and Nancy to see the Cherokee artifacts first thing the next morning, but George was dying to get a sneak preview.

"Will!" she called out when she got to the top of the escalator.

He was standing in the middle of the second-floor gallery, next to a man with cowboy boots, blow-dried brown hair, and a belt that was studded with turquoise. That had to be Seth Klein. The guy looked as if he'd stepped straight out of a magazine on the Southwest. A couple of other people were there, too, bent over a tarp in one corner of the room.

As Will turned toward her, the serious expression on his face melted into a smile. "Hey!" he said, jogging over to her. "I didn't know you were coming by."

"There must be some kind of magnetic force here," George told him. "When I got out of my last class, my feet started moving this way and they wouldn't stop."

Will grinned as she planted a kiss on his lips. "Must be my irresistible good looks," he said. "Draws women in from a radius of up to two miles."

"Oh, yeah?" George swiveled her head around expectantly. "So how come I'm the only one here?"

"Because you're the only one that counts," Will murmured, pulling her close for another kiss.

"This isn't why I came, you know," George said breathlessly when they finally pulled apart. "Did the artifacts get here all right? How's everything going?"

Will shrugged. "Hectic. Seth and I are going to be pretty busy until the show opens. Right now we're going over the layout of the gallery and figuring out what we'll need to mount the exhibit. You know—pedestals, display cases, that kind of stuff."

Glancing over her shoulder, George saw that

Seth Klein was holding a sheet of paper that looked like the gallery layout.

"Come on, I'll introduce you," Will added.

They had only taken a step or two in Seth's direction when a loud beeping noise sounded out. Seth Klein reached into his back pocket, pulled out the cellular phone, and unfolded it. "Hello?" he said. "What! They're not coming until *next* week?"

"Uh-oh," George said worriedly. "Sounds like bad news."

"Not for us, fortunately," Will told her. "Seth's got a show opening in his gallery back in Oklahoma, too." He rolled his eyes, laughing. "Sounds like it's total chaos."

Seth had let the gallery layout fall to the floor and was talking forcefully into the phone. "Call him back right away and tell him . . ."

"Are you sure he's going to have time to put *your* show together?" George whispered to Will.

"He'd better," Will said. "Seth knows what he's doing. He's just got a lot going on."

George stepped to the side as Holly Thornton and another girl came through carrying two large paintings.

"Excuse us," Holly said. When she saw George, she gave a weary smile. "Hi, George."

"How's it going?" George asked.

Holly just shrugged. "Could be better," she answered. Then she and the other girl left the gallery with the paintings.

"I feel weird," George whispered to Will. "Eileen said that Holly doesn't have any bad feelings about not getting the show, but—"

"But she's obviously not happy about it, either," Will finished, letting out a sigh. "She must have been pretty sure her proposal would be chosen. Some of the work that would have gone into her show was already stacked up here in the gallery. Holly didn't exactly jump for joy when I asked her to move it out."

George gave a rueful shake of her head.

Suddenly he grabbed her arm and steered her toward the rear of the gallery. "Come on. As long as Seth's still on the phone, I might as well show you the artifacts."

George grinned at him. "I thought you'd never ask."

CHAPTER 5

Jake's eyes scanned the crowd at the Bumblebee Diner as he and Nick went inside. There was no reason to think that Nancy would be eating a late lunch in downtown Weston, but it didn't hurt to check.

He let out a sigh as his eyes finished making a sweep of the room. No luck.

"Double cheeseburger, fries, and a triple-thick milkshake," Nick said, breaking into Jake's thoughts. "On you."

"Whatever," Jake agreed. "You really saved me this afternoon, buddy. I owe you."

"That's for sure." Nick sat down at a rear booth and propped his elbows on the scarred Formica tabletop. "Remind me never to spend another afternoon driving around with you."

Jake grabbed a plastic-coated menu from its

holder and opened it up. "It was an emergency. Helping the needy."

"After listening to you sing along with the country-western station, *I'm* the one who's needy," Nick insisted. "I need a new room-mate."

"What? You don't like my voice?" Jake asked, pretending to be insulted.

"Don't take it personally, but you sound like a record that's been melted over the radiator," Nick told him.

"That's really low," Jake said.

Nick laughed. "Since when did you turn into such a Boy Scout, anyway?" he asked.

"Since today. No big deal," Jake said, shrugging.

"Must be Nancy's influence," Nick decided. "Meet someone new, and all of a sudden she's got you helping old ladies across the street and finding homes for lost puppies."

Hearing Nancy's name made Jake want to see her even more. "No such luck," he said. "I haven't even had time to *call* Nancy today, much less actually see her. Not to mention that I still have to write a paper for one of my classes."

With all the stuff he had to do, he didn't know when he and Nancy would be able to spend time together. He just hoped it would be soon.

"The artifacts are being stored back here," Will told George as he led her to the alcove at the back of the gallery.

Until he'd seen her face at the entrance to the gallery, he hadn't realized how much he wanted to see her. Now he suddenly wanted to show her everything at once—as if the artifacts were important to understanding who he was.

"I think one of the reasons I wanted to have this show is so you could see the artifacts," he admitted.

"Me?" George asked, a curious glimmer in her eyes.

Will nodded. "So you can see where I come from. What the Cherokee culture is about."

He broke off when he stepped into the back hallway and saw that the door to the storeroom stood slightly ajar. "That's weird," he said.

"What?" George asked, frowning. "Is something wrong?"

"It should be locked. It *was* locked," Will said.

He vaulted the last two steps to the door and pushed it open, then bent over the nearest box. In a flash he spotted the feathers, shells, and horsehair of a ceremonial peace pipe. He went quickly to each of the other six boxes, checking the contents: split-cane woven basket, "buffalo man" mask, beaded moccasins and shoulder bag, buckskin robe, soapstone figure. Only when he got to the last box, containing a clay cooking pot, did he let out the breath he'd been holding.

"It's all here," he said.

"You're sure?" George stepped into the room, looking around with sober brown eyes.

Will nodded. "Positive. But I still don't understand how—"

"So *here's* where the party is," Seth Klein spoke up from the doorway. "I thought Will just disappeared on me. But seeing the company, I can understand why." He smiled at George, holding out his hand to her as he came into the storeroom. "Hi. I'm Seth Klein."

"George Fayne," George told him.

Will looked up at Seth, still feeling a little nervous. "We found the storage room door open just now. You were back here a while ago. Did you remember to lock it?"

"I was back here checking to see if there were any pedestals." Seth rubbed his chin thoughtfully, then gave a sheepish shrug. "I was talking to Kelly ..."

"His assistant," Will explained to George.

He stifled a sigh. Until that second, he hadn't minded that Seth spent so much time on the phone with his gallery in Oklahoma. But if taking care of business at home was going to make him flake out here at Wilder ...

"Wilder University is responsible for the artifacts while they're here," Will told Seth. "The head of the World of Art faculty committee put it in writing in a contract with Dan. He'll kill me if anything happens to the stuff."

"Say no more." Seth held up his hands, shooting Will an apologetic glance. "I should have known better. I promise, I'll be more careful from now on."

Seth's smile was so infectious that Will couldn't stay annoyed. "Thanks," he said.

As Seth headed for the storeroom door, the sleeve of his denim shirt caught on one of the hooks that stretched along one wall. He pulled the fabric free, then shot a look over his shoulder at George and Will. "If you need me, I'll be working on the layout for the show back in the gallery," he told them.

"I don't want to get in the way," George said to Will after Seth disappeared into the hall. "I mean, isn't there a lot to do? Shouldn't you go with him?"

"In a minute," he told her. "*After* I show you the artifacts."

George reached over to ruffle his hair. "And here I thought coming back here was just an excuse to get me alone," she teased.

"That, too," Will murmured. "That, too."

Brrring!

Bess reached out a hand and groped blindly for her alarm. She hit the button, then fell back against her pillow with a groan. Six-thirty? In the morning? Who in their right mind gets up that early?

Then she remembered. Breakfast with George, Nancy, and Will. She *had* to get up now if she wanted to have enough time to meet them and see the Cherokee artifacts before her first class.

With a sigh Bess opened her eyes and swung

her feet out of bed. "Leslie?" she asked, blinking in surprise.

Her roommate was sitting at her desk, bent over one of her texts. No big surprise there. Leslie put in more study time than anyone Bess could think of. But she was wearing the same chinos and turtleneck shirt she'd had on the night before. They actually looked rumpled. And her brown ponytail had lost its usual military precision. That was surprising.

"That was still my name, last time I checked," Leslie said in a tight, cutting voice. When Leslie turned around, Bess saw that there were dark circles under her eyes. Half a dozen paper cups of take-out coffee were lined up on her desk, as if she'd been drinking them, one by one, all through the night.

"Did you pull an all-nighter?" Bess asked groggily.

"Some of us have to study, you know," Leslie said curtly. "If I want to ace calculus, I've got to work overtime." With that, she hunched back over her notes and began scribbling furiously.

"*You're* having trouble in calculus?" Bess asked, gaping at her.

Leslie let out an irritated sigh. "Do you mind?"

"Sorry," Bess apologized. As she went to her closet and pulled out her bathrobe, she couldn't help throwing another look at her roommate. Leslie seemed to be erasing half of what she wrote, working and reworking her problem so much that she had made a hole in the paper. Her foot was jiggling a mile a minute, as if it had a tiny motor attached to it.

"Maybe you should get some rest, Leslie," Bess suggested tentatively.

Leslie sat bolt upright. "Why don't you learn to take care of yourself before you start criticizing other people!" she snapped.

Whoa! thought Bess. Where did *that* come from? "I was just trying to—"

"Well, don't," Leslie cut in. "Just keep your stuff out of my way, okay?"

Bess looked around the room. She'd cleaned up her half of the room just the night before, or at least shoved her stuff out of sight. But then she saw her boots, angled one on top of the other in the middle of the room. "Sorry. I guess I forgot to put these away before I went to sleep."

"Shhhh!"

With a sigh, Bess picked up the boots and pushed them under her bed. Leslie wasn't writing anymore. She was glowering down in frustration at the piece of paper. The foot was still going. Just looking at it made Bess tired.

It was hard not to be intimidated by Leslie. But lately Bess felt something new every time she was with her roommate.

Worry. Worry that Leslie was in some kind of trouble.

"Hey, Cody, are you all right?"

Paul Cody looked up from the *Wilder Times*

he'd been flipping through as he sat at Zeta's scarred dining room table. His roommate, Emmet Lehman, was standing in the kitchen doorway, staring at him. Emmet's eyes were barely open, and his light brown hair stuck out in a million directions.

"Why wouldn't I be all right?" Paul asked. "I'm not the one who was up half the night studying."

"True." Emmet shot a glance at Paul's coffee, toast, and newspaper. "It's just that I've never seen you this civilized. Sitting down for breakfast—with the newspaper."

"Someone else was reading the cereal box," Paul said, keeping a straight face. "This was all I could find."

"Ah. That explains it." Emmet turned and headed into the mound of dirty dishes, coffee mugs, and stale toast that passed as the frat's kitchen. "By the way, Bess called," he tossed back, as if it were an afterthought.

Paul jolted to attention. "She did? Why didn't you say so in the first place?"

Emmet shrugged. "You're on for tonight," he said, without bothering to turn around. "Pick her up at her dorm at seven."

"Yes!" Paul grinned to himself. Things were definitely starting to look up—at least where Bess was concerned.

Too bad he wasn't having as much luck in some other areas of his life.

"Hey, Emmet," he called out. "Doesn't it ever

bother you that Zeta is known almost exclusively as a party frat?"

"This is a problem?" Emmet asked, looking at him as if he'd lost his mind. "We work hard to keep that rep."

"Typical jock mentality," Paul said, shaking his head.

"I'll be sure to tell the other guys on the football team you said that. I'm sure they'll understand," Emmet said sarcastically. "Come on, Paul. Partying is what being a Zeta is all about."

"Yeah, but . . ." Paul hadn't questioned the frat's party reputation, either—until a Zeta brother got busted for dealing drugs at the beginning of the semester. "It can't hurt to get involved in some other campus things, maybe some charities."

Emmet didn't exactly seem thrilled by the idea. "I guess," he said unconvincingly.

"There have to be some worthwhile causes around." Paul jabbed a finger at a boxed-in ad in the paper. "How about the Animal Rescue League? Maybe we could volunteer for them," he suggested.

"We have enough untamed animals on our hands around here," Emmet pointed out.

"Okay, bad choice," Paul admitted. "What about"—his eyes scoured the newspaper—"the Society for World Peace."

"Too serious," Emmet said, shaking his head. "What about the society for Rowdiness and General Merriment? Do we have one of those?"

Paul rolled his eyes. This wasn't exactly going the way he'd hoped it would. "No."

"Too bad. Now, *there's* a cause I could get behind," Emmet said.

"I give up," Paul said, throwing up his hands. "Forget it. Forget I said anything."

Emmet was one of the more serious Zetas. If this is the way *he's* reacting, thought Paul, I'm going to have to look for help somewhere else.

"Here we are," George announced as she, Will, Nancy, and Bess arrived at the Kaplan Center for the Arts. "I can't wait for you guys to see the artifacts," she told Nancy and Bess. "They're really beautiful."

"Mmm." Nancy looked around distractedly at the modern white building as she stepped through the doors and into a foyer.

"Nancy?"

George was standing at the foot of an escalator, looking at her expectantly. Will and Bess were already riding up toward the second floor.

"Are you okay?" George asked.

"I guess," Nancy said. She sighed and headed toward the escalator, stepping on behind George. "I haven't seen Jake in a few days. I'm going through withdrawal, that's all."

George laughed, her brown eyes sparkling. "Nancy, you just saw Jake Wednesday night, right? That was only a little over a day ago."

"Only?" Nancy echoed, shooting her a look of mock horror.

"I know what you mean," George confided. "Sometimes I feel as if I want to spend every second with Will."

"I guess I should try to look on the bright side," Nancy said. "If I miss him this much, things *must* be really good between us."

"Tell me something I don't already know," George said, grinning.

When they got off the escalator, Nancy and George joined Will and Bess in the entrance of a wide open gallery space.

"This is the place," Will said.

"Where are the artifacts?" Bess wanted to know.

George started toward an alcove at the back of the gallery. "This way," she said.

Nancy followed the others through the alcove to a hallway that ran behind the gallery. Will and George both stopped short, in front of an open door there.

"Not again," Will said under his breath.

Nancy felt a tinge of worry in the back of her mind. "What happened?" she asked.

"Seth left the storeroom open yesterday," George explained to her and Bess. "Looks like the same thing happened today."

Nancy started to relax. Will didn't seem too worried, so everything was probably okay.

"I can't believe that guy," Will said, exasperation in his voice. Going inside the storeroom, he flicked on the light and went over to the closest box. When he bent over it, his face went gray. "Oh, no!"

"What?" Bess asked worriedly. "What is it?"

Will jumped to the next box, then the next, and the next. "They're empty!" he cried. "The artifacts are gone!"

CHAPTER 6

Gone?" Nancy stepped into the storeroom and looked into the cardboard box Will was hovering over. Sure enough, there was nothing inside except packing peanuts and protective plastic bubble wrap.

Will went quickly down the line of boxes, peeking into each. After he looked inside the last one, he sat back on his heels and sank his head in his hands. "All seven pieces," he groaned. "My life is over."

"This is awful!" George breathed, going pale.

"Hey, don't panic," Nancy said quickly. "Maybe there's a reason the artifacts aren't here."

"Like maybe someone just happened to break in and borrow them for show-and-tell?" Will suggested, cracking a strained smile.

"It's possible some art majors could have taken

them," Bess added. "You know, to study them, for inspiration maybe."

It didn't sound completely off the wall, but Nancy could tell Will wasn't taking the idea seriously. "What about Seth Klein? Could he have taken the artifacts somewhere?" she asked.

"He would have said something to me," Will said, shaking his head.

"Besides, Seth has a key," George added, examining the door. "He wouldn't have to break in. Take a look at this."

Turning to the door, Nancy saw that there were scrape marks around the lock's cylinder. "I see what you mean. Someone definitely jimmied it open."

"I can't believe this happened!" Will burst out. "I mean, I was just here. I stopped by on the way to meet you guys for breakfast and everything was fine."

He rolled his eyes toward the ceiling, then blinked in surprise. "Hey, maybe you were right about those art majors, Bess. Looks like someone's been doing a little creative work."

Following Will's gaze, Nancy saw that a metal security camera was mounted to the wall over the door. A small red light was on, showing that the camera was operating. But a messy splotch of red spray paint covered the lens and spilled onto the wall behind.

"Uh-oh," Bess said. "So much for catching the whole thing on film."

Will let out a deep sigh. "Speaking of which, we'd better call campus security."

"I'll take care of it," Bess offered. "I think I saw some phones down in the foyer."

As Bess ran from the storeroom, George went over to Will and slipped an arm around his shoulders. "Being in here is just going to make us more depressed. We might as well wait out in the gallery," she said.

Nancy started to leave the storeroom, then felt her shirt catch on one of the brass hooks that ran along the wall next to the door.

"Attack of the Killer Hooks," George deadpanned. "That happened to Seth Klein yesterday, too."

"Talk about deadly." Nancy laughed. "You need self-defense training just to get in and out of this place in one piece."

As she pulled her shirt free, a scrap of fabric fluttered to the floor. "What's this?" she murmured, bending to pick it up. The fabric was blue with distinctive black swirls on it. It was frayed around the edges.

"Looks like it ripped from someone else's shirt," George said, looking over Nancy's shoulder.

"Maybe the person who took the artifacts?" Will said thoughtfully.

"It's a pretty distinctive design," Nancy said. "Can you guys think of anyone who owns a shirt made out of that material?"

"There must be what, ten thousand students at

Wilder?" George said, giving her a sideways look. "What are we supposed to do, memorize the entire wardrobe of every single person?"

"For starters," Nancy answered, grinning. But her smile faded when she saw Will. He was staring into one of the empty boxes, his head cradled in his hands. She could only guess at what was going through his mind. "I'm really sorry this happened, Will," she said.

"Me, too," he said, looking over at her. "Me, too."

Bess tiptoed into the psych lecture hall, hoping no one would notice her. She'd spent so much time at Kaplan that she had already missed over half the class. But she didn't dare skip the whole thing. She couldn't take the chance of letting her grades slip again.

"Hey, Bess!"

Bess cringed when she heard Brian's loud hiss. But at least he was sitting near the door. She hurried down the aisle and slipped into the seat next to his.

"Slept through the snooze alarm, huh?" Brian guessed, grinning at her.

"I wish," Bess whispered back. "Actually, I've been over at Kaplan. I'll tell you about it after class. Now quick, let me see your notes so I can get a clue to what this lecture's about!"

When the class ended, she flipped her notebook shut and headed for the exit with Brian.

"So tell me," Brian said, "what was going on

at Kaplan that made you so late?" He leaned closer and gave her a conspiratorial smile. "A secret rendezvous with Paul?"

Bess made a face at him, pushing her way through the doors to the courtyard of the quad. "I barely have time for an *official* rendezvous, much less a secret one," she told him. "Actually, I was at Kaplan with Will, George, and—"

"Excuse me!" a voice called out.

Bess was jostled to the side as someone barreled past from behind, knocking the notebook from her hand. "Hey!" Bess cried.

Then she blinked at the girl. There was no mistaking the straight, rigid way she carried herself. That could only be her roommate.

"Leslie!" Bess called out. "Hello!"

Leslie was already a dozen feet ahead of her and Brian. She paused in the courtyard and glanced at them with frantic, harried eyes. "Oh. Hi, Bess. Brian."

At least she'd changed her clothes and brushed her hair. But she still looked completely exhausted.

"Hi," Brian said, giving Leslie a friendly wave. "Nice, uh, running into you this way."

Bess couldn't help laughing, but Leslie didn't seem to even have heard him. "I'm late for class," she said, biting her lip. " 'Bye." Then she turned and hurried off ahead of them.

"The next class doesn't start for another ten minutes," Brian said. "Isn't she going a little overboard on punctuality?"

Bess thought about the all-nighters Leslie had been pulling, the frantic studying and constant bad moods. "That's not all she's going overboard on," Bess said, following Leslie with worried eyes. "You don't know the half of it."

"Here's your coffee," George said to Will late Friday morning.

Will looked up from the table at Java Joe's as George and Nancy came over from the coffee bar, carrying three cups.

"Double espresso," Nancy added. "Guaranteed to keep you buzzing for hours."

"Thanks," Will said. He tried to smile, but all he really felt like doing was crawling under a rock.

"So, now what?" George asked, stirring her caffe latte.

Nancy shrugged and took a sip of her own latte. "We already talked to the security guard at Kaplan, not that it did us much good."

"That's for sure," Will scoffed.

They'd found the guard just returning to his office after making his morning rounds. He'd been gone for about an hour, so he hadn't been watching the monitors when the camera in the storeroom was spray-painted. "The guard didn't see anything. But, hey, we did get to watch a couple of fascinating security tapes."

"I especially liked the part where the hand holding the spray-paint can appeared, and then

the screen went blank," George said dryly.
"Very dramatic."

"And that security tape of the front entrance,"
Nancy added. "It was kind of existential. Lots of
cement, a few people coming in, a few going
out."

"But no one holding anything big enough to
hide the artifacts," Will finished miserably. "I
think we have to face it. The artifacts are gone."

Nancy licked the frothy milk from her spoon,
shaking her head. "Not necessarily. The police
are still at Kaplan. The artifacts could still turn
up there."

"Maybe," Will said, but personally, he
doubted it.

Campus security and the Weston police were
searching through the entire arts center, but Will
didn't have much faith that they'd find anything.
It didn't look as if they had much to go on, except that scrap of black-and-blue cloth. Will had
wanted to stay at Kaplan and look around more
himself, but the police hadn't wanted anyone else
there while they were investigating.

Will downed his double espresso in two gulps,
then let out a deep sigh. "Well, I can't put it off
any longer," he said. "I've got to call."

"Dan Chekelelee?" George guessed.

Will nodded. "And Seth Klein. Actually, I'm
kind of surprised Seth didn't show up at Kaplan
when we were there. He told me yesterday he'd
show up today by midmorning, and it was after
eleven when we left."

"Well, good luck." George gave him an encouraging smile. But as Will headed for the phones at the back of the coffee bar, he felt as if he were heading to his doom.

"How did it go?" George asked as Will slumped into the chair next to her twenty minutes later.

Even before he answered, George could tell he was still upset. Not that she blamed him. She was still half in shock herself.

"Dan didn't say much," Will explained. "Just that we shouldn't lose hope, that maybe the police will find the stuff." He took a deep breath, then let it out slowly. "*I'm* the one who screwed up, and here he was giving *me* a pep talk."

It broke George's heart to see him looking so upset. "Hey, it's not *your* fault the artifacts were stolen," she said, but she could tell he didn't agree with her.

"Dan mentioned one other thing, too," Will said. "They're not going to ship the rest of the artifacts unless the ones that were stolen are found. They can't take the risk of losing the other things, too. I guess that was his way of saying that they can't trust me."

Will's last sentence came out so quietly that George could barely hear it.

"Don't be so hard on yourself," Nancy said. "What about Seth Klein? Did you talk to him?"

Will frowned darkly, running a hand through his straight, dark hair. "I tried to. The receptionist at the Weston Inn said that he left before seven this morning and said he'd be out all day."

"Before seven?" George echoed. "But he didn't show up at Kaplan. So where'd he go?"

Will just gave a helpless shrug. "He never gave me his cell phone number, so I can't call him. I want to trust him, but . . ."

"You think he made a detour to Kaplan this morning and took the artifacts?" Nancy asked. "But we didn't see him on the security tape of the main entrance."

"There are other entrances. We didn't watch every single security tape there," Will pointed out. He shook his head. "He said something yesterday. I didn't think anything special about it at the time, but . . ."

"What?" George asked. She had a hard time believing that Seth Klein could be so devious. He seemed so open and easygoing.

"Well, he made a comment about how wealthy collectors would pay a fortune for the artifacts, if only they were for sale," Will said. "He even said something about doing anything to get the commission. I thought he was joking."

"But now the artifacts are gone *and* he's not around," Nancy finished. "So maybe he stole them and is planning to sell them on the black market?"

"The lock was jimmied, remember," George said, thinking back. "I thought you said Seth has a key."

Will just shrugged. "He could have made it

look like he'd broken the lock, so that no one would think that he was responsible."

It was possible, but something about the theory still seemed off to George. "Dan Chekelelee wouldn't send someone up here who isn't trustworthy. Didn't you say that he and Seth have worked together for years now?"

"Yeah," Will answered. His eyes were dark, moody pools of doubt. "But maybe Dan doesn't know Seth as well as he thinks he does."

Will's whole body slumped forward as he leaned his elbows on the table. "I called the World of Art jury committee, too," he went on. "I figured I might as well get all the bad news at once."

George had been so busy worrying about finding the artifacts that she'd totally forgotten about the exhibit. "And?" she asked, exchanging a worried glance with Nancy.

"They're going to wait a few days before they make any decisions about the show," Will said, staring down at the table. "But let's face it, no artifacts, no show."

"Well ..." George let her voice trail off. She wanted to tell Will something encouraging. That the artifacts would be found. That there wasn't anything to worry about.

But she knew the words would sound so empty, she couldn't bring herself to say them.

The truth was, there was plenty to worry about.

After dropping off Brian in front of the library, Bess headed toward Java Joe's for a cappuccino.

She was almost there when she spotted Holly Thornton on the mall ahead of her.

"Holly!" Bess called.

Holly was walking at such a fast clip that her long, blond hair flew out behind her. Hearing Bess's voice, she turned around and smiled. "Hi. You're not going to believe what just happened," Holly said.

"Some fox of an actor just called and asked you to costar in his next movie?" Bess guessed.

Holly let out a laugh that lit up her entire face. "No," she said. "But this is almost as good."

Bess was a little surprised to see Holly so excited. She would have expected her to be a lot more down, after not being chosen for the World of Art exhibit.

"I can hardly believe it," Holly bubbled on. "Yesterday, I thought my chances of ever working for Double Negative Design were completely gone. Now, just like that, I have another shot at it."

"What happened?" Bess asked.

"I was in my studio this morning when the police came around, asking questions about Will's stolen artifacts." Holly stopped and looked at Bess. "You heard about the theft?"

Bess nodded sadly.

Holly touched her arm. "I really am sorry for Will. I hope they find who took the art pieces and get them back," she said. Bess thought she sounded sincere.

"Anyway, then the head of the World of Art

jury committee tracked me down," Holly continued. "She said I should be prepared to mount my show, in case the police don't find the artifacts."

Bess wanted to be happy for Holly. But it was weird that her big chance came at Will's expense.

As Holly opened the door to Java Joe's, her smile faltered. "I really do feel awful about Will, though," she told Bess.

"Me, too," Bess agreed. Her eyes skimmed over the coffee bar as she stepped inside after Holly.

"You can tell him yourself if you feel like it," Bess said, pointing to a table near the windows. "Will's right over there, with Nancy and George."

Holly hesitated, looking uncomfortable. But then she unzipped her jacket and headed toward the table with Bess.

"Hi, you guys," Bess said. She looked around at her friends, then guessed, "The police haven't found the artifacts yet, huh?"

"I heard about what happened," Holly added. "I'm really sorry, Will. I can't believe someone would do that to you."

"Well, they did," he said, letting out a bitter laugh.

Holly shook her head and tucked a strand of hair behind her ear. "It's weird. I mean, I was in my studio at Kaplan all morning. I didn't have any idea of what had happened until the cops came around asking questions."

"You were there?" Will asked, sitting up straighter. "Did you see anything?"

Holly shook her head. "I was working on a design project. Anyway, I hope they find the stuff and catch whoever took it."

"Thanks," Will said.

"Well, see you," Holly said.

Bess didn't miss the way Will's eyes bored into Holly while she went over to the coffee bar and ordered.

"Why didn't it occur to me before?" Will said, tapping his forehead with the heel of his hand. "Seth's not the only one who could have a reason to take the artifacts."

Bess couldn't believe it, but Nancy actually nodded, as if the idea made sense. "She could have guessed that if your show couldn't go on, hers would probably be chosen," Nancy said. "After all, most people thought her show would be chosen in the first place."

"Hold it," Bess said, holding up her hands. "We're talking about *Holly,* remember? The vice president of my sorority?"

"She could have a reason for wanting to ruin Will's show," George pointed out. "Eileen told me yesterday that she had a summer job offer that hinged a lot on getting the World of Art show."

"Oh, yeah?" Will looked over his shoulder at Holly again. "Some people will do anything to get on the right career track," he said.

Bess shook her head firmly. "Not Holly," she

insisted. But obviously her words weren't sinking in.

"Getting the World of Art show was very important to her," Nancy said. She looked soberly around the table before adding, "The question is, would she go as far as stealing irreplaceable Native American artifacts in order to get what she wants?"

CHAPTER 7

"No way," Bess said automatically. It made her skin crawl to hear her closest friends talk about Holly this way. "She's an honest person."

Holly was just turning away from the bar, holding a take-out container of coffee. She glanced their way, and Will waved her over to them.

"Don't say anything," Bess begged him. "Please don't—"

"I hear you might get a job with Double Negative Design this summer," Will said when Holly reached their table.

Holly gave him an uncertain glance. "Maybe," she said slowly.

"Your show will probably be chosen, now that mine's basically been canceled," Will continued. "You must be pretty happy about that, huh?"

Probably? Will obviously didn't know that the World of Art jury committee had already contacted Holly, thought Bess. And I'm definitely *not* going to be the one to tell him.

"Happy?" Holly echoed. Bess could see the light blink on in her head as she realized what Will was getting at. "You don't actually think that I'd—"

"If the job is important enough to you, you might do just about anything to get it, wouldn't you?" Will challenged.

"Will . . ." Bess said, but neither Will nor Holly paid the least attention to her.

Holly faced off with him, her eyes flashing angrily. "For your information, my show *is* going up if your artifacts aren't found," she said. "But if you're trying to say that I'd *steal* to make that happen, then you obviously don't know anything about me!"

With that, she turned and stormed to the door.

"Holly, wait!" Bess called after her.

Holly didn't even slow down. As she opened the door, she shot a hurt look over her shoulder, right at Bess. Then she was gone.

Bess groaned. "Great." Everyone in Java Joe's was looking at them. She wished that she could melt into the floor and disappear. "How could you do that, Will?"

Will took a deep breath and let it out slowly. "I'm sorry. I know you're friends, but—"

"Holly didn't steal the artifacts. I know she didn't," Bess insisted. "Besides, she's not the only other World of Art finalist."

"That's right," Nancy said. "What about the third person? What's his name again?"

"Frank Chung," George supplied. "He wanted to exhibit his family's private collection of Chinese art."

"Right! Frank Chung," Bess said, clutching at the name as if it were a life preserver. Anything to get her friends to stop talking about Holly this way. "He has just as much of a reason to want to steal the artifacts as Holly."

"Maybe," George said. "He could have thought *his* show would be chosen as the replacement, not Holly's."

Bess looked hopefully at Will. "Come on," she begged. "You have to at least admit that it's possible."

"I'll give you 'possible,' " Will said after a moment. "But I'd be happier if I knew it was definite."

Something about his tone made Bess wary. He was getting at something. She just didn't know what it was. "What do you mean?" she asked.

Will crossed his arms over his chest and gave her a searching look. "How about if you took a look around Holly's room at the sorority?"

"You mean, spy on her?" Bess squeaked out, looking to Nancy and George for help.

"That *would* be one way of helping to rule her out as the thief," Nancy said slowly.

"But if you decide not to," George added, "we totally understand."

Bess gulped. She wanted to help Will recover

the Cherokee artifacts. But sneak around behind Holly's back? She just didn't know if she could bring herself to do it.

Nancy bit down on her sandwich as she hurried down the mall toward the academic quad. She'd already skipped one class that day. But she had journalism that afternoon, and that was one class she was determined not to miss.

Thank goodness for take-out food, she thought.

With so much going on, she hadn't even thought about lunch until it was time to leave for class. Luckily, Java Joe's had a supply of sandwiches and muffins that were as awesome as their coffee.

She went down a mental list of all she needed for class. Notebook, journalism text, first draft of her article on Helping Hands. It was pure luck that she'd thought to throw it all in her backpack before leaving her dorm that morning.

"Nancy?" a guy's voice interrupted her thoughts.

She turned, an expectant smile on her lips. Jake's name was halfway out of her mouth before she realized it wasn't him.

Unfortunately.

"Hi, Paul," she said, shaking herself. "How's it going?"

Paul Cody was heading the same way she was, a notebook under his arm. His square face looked more thoughtful than Nancy had ever seen it.

"Not bad," he said, "considering I live with a bunch of bozos who can't take anything seriously."

"The Zetas, huh? Actually, I heard that being serious is a crime at your frat," Nancy said, grinning.

"Punishable by strictly enforced partying," he shot back with a weak smile. "But I thought I could get the guys to branch out just a little. Maybe do some volunteer work or something."

"Save the whales?" Nancy supplied.

"Haven't seen too many of those in the Midwest lately," Paul deadpanned. "But you get the idea."

"Well, if I come up with any ideas . . ."

"Let me know. I'm desperate." Paul glanced at his watch, then loped up the steps to the quad. "Whoops! I'm almost late for econ. See you!"

" 'Bye."

Nancy turned and headed toward the ivy-covered stone building opposite the one Paul had gone into. She'd taken only a few steps when someone else called out to her.

"Nancy?"

This time it *was* Jake. Nancy whirled around, grinning when she saw him coming up the stairs behind her. His shirttails flapped out from beneath his jeans jacket, and his face was red from being outside. Nancy couldn't believe how cute he looked.

"I've been dying to see you," he said, a smile spreading across his face. He ran up the steps and caught her up in a hug that made her forget they'd ever been apart.

"Likewise," she murmured into his shoulder. It

felt unbelievably good to be in his arms. "Don't move," she told him. "Not until I've memorized what this feels like."

"Any time you need a refresher course, just call me," he said, chuckling.

As he stepped back, Nancy crinkled up her nose, sniffing the air. "What's that smell?" she wondered aloud. It was earthy, pungent.

"Smell?" Jake looked confused for a moment. "Oh, right," he said, snapping his fingers. "Kind of like a barnyard?"

Nancy nodded. "Where've you been?"

Jake's eyes lit up with pleasure. "Actually, I've been—"

He broke off as the clock tower chimed one o'clock. "Oh, no. I'm late for my last class, and I've already missed all my other classes today!"

He gave Nancy a quick kiss, then sprinted for the doorway. "Catch you later!"

"How much later?" Nancy called out good-naturedly, but he had already disappeared inside.

As she followed, Nancy realized that she hadn't had a chance to tell Jake about the stolen Cherokee artifacts. Or even to make a plan to see him over the weekend.

"Oh, well," she said under her breath. "I guess that's college life."

"What do you think?" Bess held up a deep blue, scoop-necked chenille sweater for George's opinion. It was Friday afternoon, and Bess was looking at different outfits, trying to decide on something for her date with Paul later.

"I could wear it with my black mini, ribbed wool tights, and my ankle boots," Bess said.

"Definitely," George agreed, sitting back on Bess's bed. "Not that Paul cares. You could show up for your date in a paper bag, and he'd still think you were a knockout."

"Well, with the right accessories . . ." Bess grinned, but George had the feeling that she was trying a little too hard to be upbeat.

Finally Bess put the sweater down and said, "I keep hoping that when Will sees Seth Klein, they'll straighten everything out and the artifacts will magically reappear."

"And I keep wishing I'm going to win the lottery," George said.

"Is that your way of saying I'm being unrealistic?" Bess asked.

"Just hopeful," George told her. "Anyway, at least we know where Seth is now. He didn't skip town or anything."

Will had gotten a frantic message from Seth when he called into his answering machine from Java Joe's. Apparently, Seth had arrived at Kaplan to find the artifacts missing and the Weston police still poking around the storeroom. As soon as he got the message, Will hurried over to the arts center to find Seth and explain everything.

"Maybe they *will* work everything out," Bess said. She held up a hand before George could open her mouth. "I know, I know. I'm being hopeful again."

George laughed and picked up a long flowered skirt that lay in a heap on her bed. "How about this with the sweater instead of the black mini-skirt?" she suggested.

Bess considered it for a moment, then shook her head. "I think I'll go with the short black," she decided.

"You're the fashion hound," George said, deferring.

She knew Bess didn't need any help picking out the perfect thing to wear for her date. But George didn't feel right about just leaving Bess, after what had happened at Java Joe's. Now seemed as good a time as any to talk about it.

George leaned back against Bess's pillow, then took a deep breath and said, "Sorry about what happened at Java Joe's. Will wasn't exactly as tactful as he could have been."

Bess frowned as she bent to pick up the pile of sweaters, leggings, and skirts that lay discarded on the floor. "That's okay," she finally said. "I mean, if I didn't know Holly, I might think that she took the artifacts, too."

George knew that Bess was waiting for her to say that she would vouch for Holly's honesty. But somehow, George couldn't quite do it. Holly seemed like a totally honorable person. But George couldn't rid her mind of the tiny, niggling thought that Holly had a reason to steal the artifacts.

"I'm just sorry if this makes things weird for you at the sorority," George said.

"Yeah," Bess said, giving her a funny look. "Me, too."

She dumped the pile of clothes on her bed and grabbed some books from her desk. "We'd better go. My bio class starts in half an hour, and I want to stop at the Student Union first to get some yogurt."

At the mention of food George's stomach began to growl. "I'll second that."

When the two girls got to the Student Union ten minutes later, George sniffed the air. "Mmm. French fries. Want to split some?"

"I'm on a diet," Bess said, shaking her head firmly. "At least until after Paul and I go out tonight."

They were passing a bank of pay phones, when someone stepping away from one of the phones brushed past George. She spotted a shearling jacket and a carefully brushed mane of brown hair.

"Hey, that's Seth Klein," she murmured.

"Oh, yeah?" Bess shot a curious glance at him as he breezed through the doors and headed outside. "Will must have finished talking to him. Hey, looks like he dropped something."

A thick date book lay facedown on the ground beneath the phone Seth had been using. Bess leaned down and scooped it up, along with several sheets of paper that lay strewn on the dirty floor near it.

" 'S.K.' " George said, reading the initials on the cover. "It *is* his."

Bess started to run for the door, but George grabbed her arm. "What's the hurry? Don't you want to find out what Seth was up to this morning?"

"Why didn't *I* think of that?" Bess flipped through the pages to the current week, then slid her finger to the box for Friday. " 'Nine A.M. Borrosian Gallery, Erik Borrosian,' " she read.

"He had an appointment at a gallery?" George asked.

Bess shrugged. "Art *is* his business, but wait a minute. I just saw something."

She started flipping through the loose sheets she'd picked up. "Here it is. A letter from the Borrosian Gallery to Seth's gallery in Oklahoma City."

Looking over Bess's shoulder, George skimmed over the letter. "Check this out!" she cried. "Eric Borrosian wrote, 'I was glad to learn that you will soon have some new Cherokee arts and crafts for sale. I have a client who would pay top dollar, especially for older pieces.' "

"Oh, my gosh," Bess breathed. "You don't think—"

"That maybe Seth Klein *did* take the artifacts? And that he might have sold them to Erik Borrosian this morning?" George finished. "I don't know, but we'd better tell the police about this right away."

CHAPTER 8

N ancy?"

Nancy blinked to attention in the middle of Journalism 100. Professor McCall and every student in the class were looking right at her. She tried to think of what he'd been lecturing about, but she came up with a blank.

"Yes?" she said uncertainly.

Uh-oh. It was the first time all semester she hadn't been paying close attention. It figured that she'd get snagged.

Professor McCall gave her a frank, probing gaze. "I was talking about journalistic technique. How to go out there and find the story that will grab every reader's attention. Wouldn't you say that's every journalist's dream?"

"Sure," Nancy agreed, feeling her cheeks burn. It was *so* embarrassing to have him repeat everything he'd just been talking about, especially after he'd complimented Nancy on her article about REACH. Oh, well. That's what you get for daydreaming about your boyfriend, Nancy told herself.

"How would *you* search out a major scoop?" Professor McCall asked her.

Nancy searched her mind for techniques that were listed in their journalism text, but when it came right down to it . . . "Instinct," she said. "Keeping my eyes and ears open. Keeping up on what's going on around me. Sometimes doesn't it just come down to being in the right place at the right time?"

"And knowing what to do when that happens," McCall said, with an approving nod. "How about giving us an example?"

That was easy. Her whole morning at Kaplan was exactly what he was talking about. "Well, a friend of mine is the student curator for the premiere World of Art exhibit," she began.

"The Cherokee artifacts?" Professor McCall came around his desk and leaned against the front of it.

"Yes," Nancy answered.

In the next few minutes the story of the stolen artifacts came tumbling out. Before long, everyone in the class was joining in. They spent the rest of the class talking about how to follow the story of the missing artifacts.

By the time class was over, Nancy's head was spinning.

The discussion had reinforced everything she,

Will, George, and Bess had already been over. Dan McCall had agreed that talking to both the other World of Art finalists would be an important part of any investigative journalist's research.

But don't forget to look beyond the obvious, too, he'd said. The other two finalists may not be the only people with a reason to steal the artifacts.

Nancy had immediately thought of Seth Klein. But it was something else Dan McCall said that stuck in her mind the most.

"It's important to keep an emotional distance," the professor had advised. "If you get too close, you could miss something important."

He was talking to the whole class, of course, but Nancy felt as if his words were meant specifically for her.

After stepping outside into the cold afternoon air, she started walking resolutely toward the Kaplan Center for the Arts. She hadn't had a chance to do more than talk to the security guard and look in the storeroom earlier. She certainly hadn't been able to look around the student art studios, especially Holly Thornton's.

Nancy liked Holly. She didn't like to think that Holly could have anything to do with the artifacts being taken. But Professor McCall was right. She had to remain objective. And objectively speaking, Holly did have a reason for wanting to prevent Will's show from going up.

When Nancy got to Kaplan, she found out from the directory that the student studios were on the fourth floor. Just two flights up from the gallery and storeroom.

Hmm, thought Nancy. If Holly *had* decided to steal the artifacts, she could probably have done it without attracting much attention. If she hid the things *inside* the building, that would explain why the security camera at the entrance didn't show anyone leaving the building with the artifacts. The police were supposed to search the building, but they might have overlooked something.

The fourth floor had a raw, industrial feel to it. The floors were plain concrete, and white partitions separated the long row of studios from one another. There were splotches of paint, clay, and masking tape just about everywhere. Someone was playing music, but the sound Nancy focused on was a voice.

Holly's voice. Coming from a studio somewhere ahead.

"How many times are you going to rework this piece, B.J.?" Holly was asking. "You've got to finish it in the next few days if it's going to go in my show."

"What can I say?" a guy's voice spoke up. "When inspiration strikes, I can't ignore it."

Nancy walked toward the voices and spotted Holly standing just inside the door to a studio. A tall, lanky guy with wiry blond hair was standing in front of a sculpture made of video screens built into a framework of metal and copper wire. He seemed to be in the middle of attaching a row of video screens to the piece.

"Just do it *fast,*" Holly told the guy. "The head of the jury committee said I have to be ready to mount my show in just over a week." She seemed exasperated, excited, and nervous all at once.

Nancy took a deep breath, then stepped up to the doorway. "Hi, Holly," she said.

Holly looked surprised to see her and not too pleased. "Hi, Nancy. What are you doing here?"

"Just looking around," Nancy said. "Could we talk somewhere? Maybe in your studio?"

Holly's whole body stiffened. "Why?" she asked. "So *you* can give me the third degree, too?"

This was obviously going to be harder than Nancy had thought. "I'm just trying to help Will."

As soon as she mentioned Will's name, Holly cut in. "If you think I took those artifacts, that's your problem, Nancy," she said. "I don't have to justify my existence to you or anyone else."

"No, of course not," Nancy said quickly. "I just thought maybe you saw something. Actually, we found a scrap of fabric that could have been ripped off the shirt the person was wearing. It was bright blue, with these black squiggles on it."

As Nancy described the fabric, Holly's brown eyes flickered. Then, just as quickly, the look was gone.

"Sorry. I'm busy," Holly said curtly. She

brushed past Nancy and went down the hall, disappearing into one of the other studios.

Busy? Nancy wondered. Or simply trying to avoid me?

When she turned back around, Nancy realized that B.J. was staring at her intently.

"You've got a great face," he said. "You should think about modeling for the life drawing classes."

At first Nancy thought it was a come-on, but the look on his face wasn't at all flirtatious. "I don't think so," she said, feeling self-conscious.

Changing the subject, she pointed to the mess of wires, video screens, and metal that he was working on. "That's interesting. Does it come with instructions?"

"Is that your way of saying you don't understand what it means?" he asked, letting out a rich laugh. "By the way, I'm B. J. Olson."

"Nancy Drew," she told him, smiling. "And I guess I don't."

"Well, it's a statement about the way things work. That everything is made out of something else," B.J. explained.

B.J. pointed to the row of video screens that he was installing. "I'm going to run images of famous buildings on these screens, you know, like the Eiffel Tower . . ."

"Or the Empire State Building?" Nancy finished.

B.J. grinned at her. "Exactly."

Nancy wasn't sure she'd want the thing in her

living room at home, but B.J. was amiable enough, and he seemed to like to talk. "Looks like you've put in a lot of time working on it," she said. "Is it for the World of Art show?"

B.J. shot her a sideways glance. "You don't give up, do you?" he said. "I've already talked to the cops. You can find out from them where I was this morning when the artifacts were taken."

"Sorry," Nancy said, grimacing. "Will Blackfeather is a friend of mine, that's all."

"Being in the premiere World of Art exhibit is definitely going to look good on my résumé after I get my masters degree," B.J. said. "But I'm not the only one. About twenty other students are going to have work in Holly's show, too. There are plenty of other people to check out besides me."

"I guess so," Nancy admitted.

As she left B.J.'s studio, she let out a sigh. Thanks to *objective* reporting techniques, she now had more suspects.

About twenty more. She couldn't possibly check them all out. So, what was she going to do now?

Bess took a deep breath and stopped in front of the door to Kappa house. She'd come straight here after bio. She hoped some of what the professor had said would sink in through osmosis, because she'd been too preoccupied to pay much attention.

One thing had become clear, though. She

couldn't let Holly go on thinking that she didn't trust her. They had to talk. Squaring her shoulders, Bess opened the door and stepped into the foyer.

"Hold it right there!" a voice called out.

Bess froze, then relaxed when she realized that it was just Eileen O'Connor. She was perched on the staircase with a jumbo sketch pad open on her knees. "This'll only take a minute," Eileen said, moving her hand in deft, sweeping strokes.

"I like the element of surprise. There's just one problem," Bess said, trying not to move.

Eileen's eyes flicked back and forth between Bess and the pad. "What's that?"

"You're not going to have anyone left to draw if you give us all heart attacks," Bess said, grinning.

"Hey, stop moving. Put your mouth back the way it was, please," Eileen said.

"Okay." Bess stopped smiling. She tried to keep still, but she couldn't stop her eyes from darting to the living room, then to the hall that led to the Kappas' kitchen. "Is Holly around?" she asked.

Eileen shook her head. "She's at Kaplan," she answered.

"Oh." So much for having a heart-to-heart, Bess thought.

"Okay, you can breathe again," Eileen said. She tore the sheet of sketch paper from the pad and held it up. "Here you are. Bess Marvin, immortalized for all of my intro drawing class to see."

"Lucky me," Bess said dryly. She took a quick look at the sketch on her way up the stairs, but she wasn't paying very close attention.

When she got to the second floor, Bess stopped outside Holly's room and quickly scribbled a note in her notebook. After tearing it out, Bess folded the note and wedged it in the crack of Holly's door.

There. Even if we can't talk face-to-face, at least Holly will know how bad I feel about what Will said to her *and* that I know she'd never steal the artifacts.

As she headed back downstairs, Bess felt as if a ten-ton weight had just been lifted from her shoulders. She tried not to think about Will. He was just going to have to understand that sneaking around behind Holly's back was too much to ask.

She let out a sigh before heading out the Kappas' front door. At least, I *hope* he understands.

Soozie Beckerman watched through her open bedroom doorway as Bess stuck something in Holly's door. She'd been about to get something to drink downstairs, but first . . .

She waited until Bess disappeared down the stairs, then slipped down the hall to Holly's room. After checking to make sure that no one was around, she plucked the paper free and unfolded it.

As she skimmed the page, a satisfied smirk spread across her face. Such a touching declaration of support:

" 'I know you'd never steal anything, and I've said as much to Will. I just want you to know that I stand behind you a hundred percent. If there's been any misunderstanding between us, I hope this clears it up. . . .' "

Soozie skipped over the rest of it. She'd already seen enough. Refolding the note, she tapped it against her chin.

So, she thought, trouble brewing between Holly and her favorite little pledge, eh? This could turn out to be just the opportunity I've been waiting for.

It wasn't exactly a secret at Kappa that Soozie and Holly didn't get along. Soozie never would have thought Holly would be popular enough to become the sorority's vice president. Or that so many of Holly's freshmen "picks" for the sorority—like Bess Marvin—would be chosen to pledge.

Soozie felt her power slipping. And she didn't like it. But if she could get even one of Holly's favorites to quit . . .

Taking the note, Soozie went back down the hall to her room. She tore the note into dozens of confetti-like scraps. Scooping the bits of paper into her hand, she let them flutter to the bottom of her trash basket.

* * *

"Max? Hi, it's Nancy Drew." Nancy sat at her desk with the phone cradled between her shoulder and ear. In front of her was the first draft of her article on Helping Hands, with some questions she'd penciled in the margins. "I'm glad I caught you. Do you have a minute for some follow-up questions to our interview?"

"What else would I have to do at six o'clock on a Friday night?" Max Krauser's amiable voice came back over the line.

"It's a bad time," Nancy realized.

She felt a pang as she glanced at the two faded roses in the soda bottle on her dresser. Here it was Friday night, and she didn't even know if she and Jake would be able to spend it together.

"I'm heading out to the rally for tomorrow's football game." Max's voice broke into her thoughts. "But I can talk for a few minutes. I'm glad you called, actually. After you left the other day, I realized that I forgot to mention the big casino weekend we help out with every year. A lot of our funding comes from it."

"The Black and White Nights?" Nancy asked. She remembered Jake mentioning the casino weekend when they were out to dinner.

"So you've heard of it. That's a good sign," Max said.

"A friend of mine was talking about it," Nancy told him. She grabbed her pen and turned to a fresh page of her notebook. "What can you tell me about it?"

"Well, the first night is black tie, and reserved

for the alumni and students on the volunteer committee. That's when we make the real money. But both nights have dancing, dinner, every casino game you can think of, and entertainment," Max explained. "And the second night is for students. Less formal but definitely more fun."

Nancy's pen flew over the page as she jotted down the details. "Sounds great."

"There's just one problem," Max said. "The fundraiser's only a month away, but we've been so busy around here that I'm behind on my share of organizing. We don't have the entertainment set up yet or volunteers to help with refreshments. Stuff like that. I was hoping you could mention in the article that we need volunteers. Desperately."

"You got it," Nancy agreed. As she made the notation, she remembered what Paul Cody had said when she'd run into him.

"I might know at least one person who'd like to get involved," she told Max. "Make that two people. You can count me in, too."

"Great!" Max said.

Nancy could practically feel his smile over the line. "But for the article, should I have volunteers call the Helping Hands office?"

After talking to Max for a few more minutes, she hung up the phone. She's promised herself not to get involved with Helping Hands until after her article was done, but this was important. And anyway, the write-up *was* finished, or almost.

Through her bedroom floor, Nancy heard the pounding bassline of music from the suite below. Starting early tonight, she thought, laughing.

She looked back at her notes and was about to turn on her computer, but then she changed her mind.

It *is* Friday night, she reminded herself.

She reached for her phone and dialed Jake's number, then let out a sigh when his machine picked up. "Earth to Jake," she said after the beep sounded. "Give me a call if you think we might be in the same solar system anytime soon. This is Nancy."

She was just hanging up, when Ginny stuck her head in.

"Suite 201 just sent up a messenger," Ginny said, grinning. "Open party, starting now. Reva, Stephanie, and I are going down in a few minutes."

"Sounds good," Nancy said. "I'll be right out."

She ran a brush through her hair a few times, then left a note for Jake on her message board. Just in case, she thought hopefully.

Ginny, Stephanie, Kara, and Reva were all in the lounge when she got there.

"Reva just told us about the stuff for Will's show being stolen," Ginny said, looking concerned. "Unbelievable!"

"Andy told me about it," Reva spoke up from the sofa. Reva and Andy Rodriguez had been dating since they'd worked together to write a student guide to the Internet. Since Andy was

Will's roommate, it wasn't surprising that he'd heard about the missing artifacts.

"It must be really bad karma to steal Native American artifacts," Kara commented. "I mean, that's like disturbing a sacred spirit or something, isn't it?"

"Um, Kara? Karma is a concept associated with Asian religions," Stephanie pointed out dryly. "It doesn't have anything to do with the Native American cultures of North America."

Kara gave a breezy wave. "All I'm saying is that I wouldn't want to be whoever took that stuff. It's definitely going to come back to haunt them."

"I hope so," Nancy said.

"Andy said that Will's taking it pretty hard," Reva said. "Do the cops have any idea who did it?"

Nancy wasn't sure how much to say. Bess had called earlier to tell her that Seth Klein had a agreement to sell Cherokee art to a dealer in Chicago. And then there was Holly—she had every reason to want Will's show to be canceled. But Nancy didn't want to foul up the police investigation by spreading rumors that could turn out not to be true.

"I think they've got a couple of leads," she said vaguely. "Are you guys ready to party?"

"Yes!" Kara, Ginny, and Reva all chorused.

"As long as there's nothing better to do," Stephanie added disdainfully.

Reva shot a quick glance at Stephanie's slinky

red bodysuit. "Maybe you should skip it, Steph. We know how you hate to mingle with the opposite sex."

Stephanie opened her mouth, then closed it again as the door to their suite opened and a guy came in. He was Asian, with a short dark hair and nice eyes. He looked kind of preppy, with corduroys, and a button-down shirt under his crewneck sweater.

"Nice welcome committee," he said, grinning at the girls. "Is Ginny Yuen around?"

Ginny held up a hand. "Right here." She squeezed around Stephanie, who leaned against the wall, frankly appraising the guy.

"Here." The guy plucked a pile of fliers from his canvas shoulder bag and held one out to her. "I'm handing these out for the Asian Society. It's an announcement for our fall formal."

"I knew you looked familiar," Ginny said, smiling at him. "I remember seeing you at some of the meetings."

"Frank Chung," he said, holding out his hand. "Don't ask me why, but I volunteered to deliver all these. I've been running around campus all afternoon."

As soon as Nancy heard the guy's name, she looked at him again. Frank Chung, huh? He was the third finalist for the premiere World of Art exhibit.

"Thanks," Ginny told him, taking the flyer.

"No problem." As Frank opened the flap of his bag to put the fliers back inside, Nancy caught sight of a wad of bunched-up fabric. Bright blue fabric with black squiggles on it.

Exactly the same as the scrap that she'd found in the storeroom right after the Cherokee artifacts were stolen.

"Cool fabric," she commented, trying to get a closer look inside the bag. "What is it, a shirt or something?"

"Huh?" Frank glanced into the bag, then looked at her nervously. "Uh, yeah. Right. A shirt."

He quickly closed the flap, but not before Nancy caught a glimpse of a can of spray paint wrapped inside the fabric. She couldn't be sure, but she thought she saw splatters of red on the can and fabric. The color that just happened to be spray-painted over the security camera in the storeroom!

"What's with the sudden interest in men's fashions?" Kara asked, looking confused.

"I've got to go," Frank said before Nancy could answer. "Maybe I'll see you at the formal, Ginny."

"Maybe," Ginny replied. By the time the word was out of her mouth, Frank Chung was gone.

Stephanie watched the suite's door swing closed behind him. "Do men *always* run away from you like that?" she asked Nancy archly.

Only when they've got something to hide, Nancy thought.

CHAPTER 9

Jake looked through his car windshield at the run-down Victorian house where he, Dennis, and Nick had their apartment. For the last ten minutes he'd been honking the horn, but so far the only one who'd heard was Mrs. Pittaluga, the elderly woman who lived on the ground floor, and she hadn't looked very happy.

"Come on," Jake urged under his breath. "Nick . . . Dennis . . . where *are* you?"

"Why don't you lay on that horn a little longer?" Nick asked, appearing next to the driver's window. "I don't think anyone quite *heard* you."

"Nick, finally!" Jake cried. "Listen, old pal, old buddy . . ."

Nick started to back away, a look of distrust in his dark eyes. "Uh-oh. Something tells me I should turn around and walk the other way."

Shooting his hand out the window, Jake grabbed Nick's sleeve. "I need your help. I've been running around all day trying to take care of business."

"Speaking of which, Nancy called," Nick informed him. "Three times."

"I can't believe I missed her—again!" Jake groaned and let his head bang against the steering wheel, then jumped back as the horn blared. "Sorry, Mrs. Pittaluga!" he called out when the woman's gray-haired head appeared in one of the ground-floor windows.

"Smooth," Nick commented, cracking up. "I don't suppose you'd consider letting go of my sleeve now."

"Negative," Jake told him. "Not until you help me. I have to—"

"Oh, no," Nick interrupted, peering into the backseat of the car. "Don't tell me you've done it again."

"I've done it again," Jake said bluntly.

Nick shot him a look of disbelief. "Why me? Why don't you ask Nancy to help you?"

"I tried. Her phone was busy," Jake answered. "By the way, what did she say when she called?"

"Something about solar systems and giving her a call when you land," Nick said distractedly. He was still staring into the backseat. "Are you two having trouble or something?"

"Trouble?" Jake shook his head adamantly.

"Not a chance. Well, except I've hardly seen her at all in the last day or so."

Nick gave him a blank look.

"Every time I call her, she's out," Jake explained. Every time she calls—"

"You're busy with your new"—Nick glanced into the backseat again—"hobby."

Jake grimaced. "Which gets us back to what we're doing here in the first place," he said. He reached across to open the passenger door. "Come on. Help me take care of this. *Then* I'll call Nancy . . . again."

Ginny wove through the dense partyers who were packed into Suite 201 in Thayer Hall. She didn't have any idea where everyone else from her floor was. Nancy, Stephanie, Kara, and Reva had evaporated into the crowd as soon as they got there.

"Want to dance?"

Ginny looked up as a tall guy materialized out of a knot of other guys. His head was bobbing up and down to a song that blared from two huge speakers in the lounge.

"Thanks, but I think I'll pass," she told him.

The guy cupped his free had around his ear. "What?" he cried over the music.

Ginny raised her voice a few notches. "I said, no, thanks!"

"Whatever," the guy said, shrugging. "We can just talk, if you want. What's your name?"

"Ginny. And I really have to go."

It wasn't just a line. She'd just stopped down at the party for a minute, but now she had to go meet Ray. "Maybe I'll be back in a little while," she told him.

"Yeah? Great!" the guy said hopefully.

"With my boyfriend," Ginny finished. She squeezed past him and headed back up to her own suite.

She was just putting her key in her door when she saw it. A small white box dangling from her message board by a red ribbon. A tiny card tied to the ribbon said, Ride the magic.

"Ray," she whispered, feeling a warm glow spread through her.

Her heart started beating faster as she slipped the box from the ribbon and opened it. Inside were a pair of dangly silver earrings. A small piece of turquoise was set in the middle of each one.

"Oooh," she breathed. "How beautiful."

Hurrying into her room, she went to the mirror over her dresser and held them to her ears. The design was a little funkier than what she usually wore, but she loved the way they looked with her shiny blue-black hair flowing behind them.

"Ride the magic"—the lyrics she'd written for the Beat Poets' newest song, "Freefall."

As she looked at her reflection, it hit her. What she and Ray had *was* magic. Nothing else could explain the incredible chemistry they had.

The phone rang, and Ginny put one of the

silver earrings down so she could answer. "Hello?"

"Hello, Ginny. It's Mother."

Ginny blinked in surprise. The hand holding the other earring dropped, and the piece of jewelry landed on the dresser with a metallic *thunk*.

"Mom! Hi!" she said, a little too brightly. She didn't know why, but she suddenly felt guilty, as if her mom had caught her and Ray kissing.

"You're in a good mood," her mother said, chuckling. "Is everything going well? You're keeping up with your classes?"

"Mmm. Everything's fine," Ginny answered. She knew how important it was to her parents that she do well at Wilder. It was the first step to getting into a good medical school, the beginning of the future her parents had always wanted for her. That she had always wanted for herself.

Until Ray came along.

But now, with him and the band, there was so much more than just studying.

Ginny took a deep breath and shifted the receiver to her other ear. Tell her, she ordered herself. "Mother, there's something I have to—"

"You haven't mentioned the Asian Society lately," her mother said at the same time.

"Actually, they're having a party soon," Ginny said distractedly, her eyes falling on the flier Frank Chung had dropped off. "But I wanted to tell you—"

"That sounds lovely!" her mother broke in.

"Your father will be pleased. I don't have to tell you how important it is to keep our cultural traditions, especially now that you're away from home."

Ginny's stomach started to churn. Her mother sounded so proud and pleased. Ginny couldn't bring herself to tell her that she wouldn't even be going to the party. Or that the reason she wasn't going was that her boyfriend was playing live on the campus radio station that night in a rock-and-roll band. Her very *un*Asian boyfriend.

"Who knows?" her mother added in a conspiratorial voice. "Maybe you'll meet someone special there."

Every time her mother spoke, Ginny felt the knot in her stomach twist tighter and tighter. She knew exactly what kind of boy her mom had in mind—brilliant, preppy, a future doctor or lawyer or nuclear physicist. And Chinese. Definitely *not* a rock-and-roller from the wheat fields of Illinois.

Tell her! ordered a voice inside Ginny's head. You can't keep Ray a secret from them forever.

But she just couldn't. Not yet. "Yes, Mother," she said weakly. "Maybe I *will* meet someone."

George wrapped her arms tightly around Will's waist and buried her face against the back of his jacket. As he leaned into a curve on his motorcycle, a sharp blast of cold wind stung her cheeks. She didn't know where they were going. She didn't think even Will knew. All he'd said was

109

that he needed to blow off some steam and get as far away from Wilder University as he could.

George's fingers were freezing, but it felt good to be on the road—to be driving without thinking about what was ahead. Or about all the trouble they had left behind.

The road seemed to go on forever. Endless fields of frozen, plowed-under corn spread out in all directions. The twilight sky was threaded with red, orange, and purple ribbons. Here and there stood a farmhouse or a deserted roadside stand where vegetables were sold during the harvest season.

George didn't know what time it was when Will stopped, next to a worn, wooden stand littered with a few dried-up corn husks. For a while they just sat there with their feet dangling over the edge of the stand, holding hands and staring out at the empty fields. As the sky darkened, a few stars blinked on overhead.

"It's beautiful here." George's whisper broke the silence. "Not another person in sight."

Will gave her hand a squeeze, looking down at her with eyes filled with love. "Just like when we went camping," he said in a husky voice. "Just you, me, and the stars."

Thinking back to the camping trip, George felt her whole body buzz with electricity. That had been their first time . . . really being together. And ever since, they'd only gotten closer.

"We don't have a tent now," George pointed out.

"Or sleeping bags."

Will leaned closer to George. His mouth melted onto hers with an urgency George hadn't felt in him before. She leaned back onto the farm stand, wrapping her arms tightly around his lean, powerful torso. But after a long, passionate kiss, Will sat up abruptly and let out a sigh.

"Sorry," he said, looking out at the fields again. "I keep getting distracted."

"Could have fooled me," George said, chuckling. She sat up next to him and planted a soft kiss on his cheek. "Was it something I said?"

"You know it wasn't," he told her. "I just keep thinking about Dan Chekelelee—of how disappointed he must be in me."

Hearing the pain in Will's voice made George's heart break right in two. "It's not your fault," she reminded him. "Besides, the police are going to find the artifacts. They have to."

"Not necessarily," Will said, frowning. "What if Seth Klein already sold them to that gallery in Chicago?"

"The Borrosian Gallery," George supplied. "The police promised to check it out. But I've been thinking. If Seth stole the artifacts, why would he bother to stick around? He went to the gallery at Kaplan *and* he called you when he found the police there. I mean, if *I'd* just stolen some priceless artifacts and sold them, I'd be on the first plane out of the country."

Will gave her a weak smile and said, "Maybe Seth's not as smart as you are."

"He *does* have nice hair, though," George joked. It was a cheap attempt to cheer him up, but it worked. Will actually laughed.

"Selling the artifacts *would* give Seth enough money to keep him in hair products for a long time," he said. "Seriously, maybe he's sticking around because he thinks he can fool everyone into believing he's innocent. That way he gets to keep the money without giving up his whole life in Oklahoma."

George's head ached from going over the different possibilities so many times. Leaning against Will, she nuzzled her head against his shoulder. "My fingers are getting numb out here. I'm not sure they're even attached to my hands anymore. Why don't we go somewhere warm?"

"Sounds good," he agreed. "Somewhere warm where I don't have to think about how lousy everything is."

George looked out over the darkened cornfields, thinking. "The movies?" she finally suggested. "They're showing *Night Raiders* at one of the theaters in Weston."

Will at least looked as if he were considering it. "Not a bad idea," he decided. "Thrills, chills."

"And lots of distraction," George finished. "Come on. If we leave now, we might be able to make it."

"Wow! You look great, Bess." Paul Cody's eyes lit up when Bess appeared in the lobby of Jamison Hall at seven o'clock Friday night. If she'd had any doubts about the outfit she'd picked, the look on his face totally erased them.

"Thanks," she said, giving him a little kiss on the cheek. She glanced at the two paper bags he held, then sniffed the air. "Is that a new cologne you're wearing?" she asked.

"Eau de Cheeseburger," he said, grinning. "Like it?"

"I love it. Especially if it comes with some Eau de French Fries," she said hopefully.

"You got it!" Paul raised an eyebrow, giving her a sideways glance as they headed outside. "Fast food seemed like the safest bet for dinner," he went on. "I figure I've got five minutes, maybe ten, max, before you run off on me."

Bess shook her head firmly and slipped her hand into the crook of Paul's arm. "No way. You promised to tell me your deepest, darkest secrets, remember? I'm not going to pass *that* up," she told him. "Not to mention that I've been dying to see *Night Raiders.*"

"Me, too. Sci-fi blood and gore," he joked. "My favorites." Paul pulled his hand from his jacket pocket and twined his fingers with hers.

Bess's heart skipped a beat. "So, is sci-fi one of your secrets?" she asked, raising a teasing brow.

"The first secret, actually. I'm also totally addicted to fast food," he confided.

"Sounds like we have a lot in common," she said.

When she looked up at him, Paul's eyes were

sparkling with warmth. "And this is just the beginning."

The beginning. She wasn't sure where, exactly, things were leading, but she definitely wanted to find out.

Half an hour later they were sitting in a movie theater, watching the large screen.

"Oh, my gosh. Don't kiss her now," Bess breathed to the on-screen actor. "There's a Night Raider in the closet right next to you!"

"You know how it is when it comes to love. Common sense flies right out the window," Paul whispered. But he was looking at her, not the movie.

Bess was just turning to Paul when two people sat down in the seats in front of them. She didn't pay attention to who they were, until one of them turned around and she heard someone whispering, *"Psst! Bess!"*

"George!" Bess smiled and waved at her cousin. "Hi, Will!"

"Shhhh!" half a dozen people hissed at once.

"Ooops!" Bess clamped her mouth shut and slid as far down in her seat as she could.

"Talking during a movie is considered a capital offense in some states," Paul whispered teasingly in her ear.

Bess pretended to glare at him, but it was impossible to be stern. "Oh, my gosh! It's too quiet," she whispered, her eyes back on the screen. "That must mean they're about to attack again."

She didn't even know when Paul grabbed her hand. But suddenly he was squeezing it, and Bess felt a thrill that had nothing to do with what was happening on the screen.

A few minutes later she spotted another late arrival coming down the side of the room. As the girl passed their row, looking for a place to sit, Bess recognized Holly's willowy build and long blond hair. She leaned forward, trying to get her attention.

For a moment Holly's eyes locked on her, and Bess smiled and waved. "Hi," she mouthed.

She was sure Holly must have gotten her note by now, but the look Holly shot Bess was an angry glare. Seconds later Bess saw Holly looking at George and Will. Holly gave a low snort, then circled around to the other side of the room and sat down there.

Bess felt as if Holly had just slapped her across the face. "Whoa!" she murmured, sinking back against her chair back.

"What happened?" Paul whispered.

"Shhhhh!"

Bess shrugged helplessly at Paul. But inside, she was wondering, What *had* just happened? Was it possible that Holly *hadn't* gotten her note yet?

A flicker of movement caught Bess's attention. Will was looking over his shoulder at her. He glanced toward the other side of the room, where Holly was sitting, then looked back at Bess.

Bess had a feeling she knew what he was asking: Had she searched Holly's room yet?

She shook her head slightly, then let out a sigh when Will rolled his eyes and turned back to the screen once again.

Great, thought Bess. Now Holly *and* Will are mad at me.

CHAPTER 10

Nancy tried to dance, but the crowd in Suite 201 had gotten so dense that there was hardly any room to move.

"I give up!" she called over to Reva, who was also moving to the music. "Want something to drink?"

Reva held up a plastic cup and grinned. "Already taken care of. Thanks, anyway!" she yelled back. Her dark eyes were shining, and beads of perspiration covered the light brown skin of her forehead.

Nancy squeezed around some people, looking for anyplace the drinks might be. "Bill!" she called out, catching sight of the suite's resident adviser, Bill Graham. With his red hair and six-foot-plus build, he was impossible to miss, even in this crowd.

"Hi, Nancy," he greeted her.

He was leaning against the wall at the edge of the lounge, talking to Nancy's RA, Dawn Steiger. Nancy didn't miss the way the two looked at each other. They had definitely been spending more time together lately.

"What's up, Nancy?" Dawn said, speaking loudly above the music.

"I'm totally dehydrated," Nancy began. "Where are the—"

Bill laughed, holding up a hand. "Say no more. It got so crowded out here, I put the drinks in my room. Help yourself."

"Thanks!"

Half a dozen other people were already standing around in Bill's room. "Eileen," Nancy said, when she saw her suitemate pouring a drink. "I didn't even know you were here."

"Is there anyone who's *not* here?" Eileen laughed. She gestured to a short, slender girl with wavy black hair who was with her. "Nancy, this is Gisella. I dragged her all the way here from Kaplan. *Someone* had to make her stop working on her intro drawing project."

Gisella laughed. "Nothing like waiting until the last minute to start my drawings. I got Holly up at seven this morning and dragged her over to Kaplan. She was ready to kill me."

"Holly?" Nancy asked. "Holly Thornton?"

"Yes," Gisella nodded. "I had her cornered in her studio from eight until after nine."

Nancy blinked in surprise. "You were with her the whole time?"

"From when I woke her right up until the second she threatened to hit me over the head with her drawing table," Gisella said, laughing.

So Holly *couldn't* have stolen the Cherokee artifacts, Nancy realized. Between seven and nine was exactly when the thief had struck.

"That's great," Nancy murmured.

"What's great?" Eileen asked. "That Holly threatened Gisella?"

"Oh. No, not that," Nancy said, shaking herself. "Sorry, I was just thinking out loud."

Turning to Gisella, she asked. "You heard about the Cherokee artifacts being stolen, right? You didn't happen to see anything, did you?"

Gisella shook her head. "Not a thing. I was talking to Holly and B. J. Olson about it after the police came through. None of us saw anything."

"B.J. was there, too?" Nancy asked.

Hmm, she thought. Maybe Holly had an alibi now, but B.J. didn't.

"Sure," Gisella answered. "And it's a good thing, too. After the jury committee told Holly that she should get her show ready, B.J. really had to get to work on the piece he's going to have in it. If you ask me, it's going to be the best thing in the show."

"If he ever decides to finish it," Eileen added with a grin.

B.J. was just one of the artists who would be

exhibited. There wasn't any reason to think he'd have anything special to gain.

Was there?

Will held the telephone receiver to his ear and spoke to a detective from the Weston Police Department. "Can you tell me if there are any new developments in the investigation?" Will asked.

He heard the detective chuckle over the line. "It's a little early to be calling, isn't it?" he asked Will. "I thought college students liked to sleep late on Saturday mornings."

"If they can," Will agreed. "Unfortunately, I haven't been getting much sleep since the artifacts were taken."

He tried again to get the detective to talk about what the police had found out. "What about the Borrosian Gallery?" Will pressed.

"I sent a few men up to Chicago yesterday afternoon. They ought to be reporting in first thing today."

"George and I will be right there," Will said. "We'd like to hear what they have to say."

The detective started to say something, but Will hung up before he could get a word out. He didn't want to give the guy a chance to talk him out of it.

"Right where?" George appeared in his bedroom doorway in her oversize red T-shirt. She yawned, rubbing the sleep from her eyes. Then, limping slightly, she came through the apartment's minuscule living room to the kitchen area.

"We're going to the police station. That's the only way we're going to find out what the detectives have come up with." Taking her arm, Will steered her back toward the bedroom. "Come on. You have to get dressed."

George shot a sleepy glance at him. "Should we call Nancy? She might want to come. I doubt we can say the same for Bess, though." She paused, raising an eyebrow at him. "You weren't exactly nice to her last night."

At the mention of Bess's name, a pang of guilt hit Will. "I know. I should have just ignored that Holly was even there. If she *did* take the artifacts, it's not Bess's fault," he admitted.

"Does that mean you'll call and apologize?" George asked hopefully.

He nodded, then bent to kiss the tip of her nose. "*After* we go to the police station. Now hurry! I'll call Nancy while you get dressed."

"You and George go ahead without me, Will," Nancy whispered into the phone.

She shot a quick glance at the lump underneath Kara's blankets, but it didn't budge. Kara could be annoying, but at least she was a sound sleeper. "I still need to take a shower and get something to eat. Maybe we can meet up in a while, so you guys can fill me in?"

"Let's see . . . I've totally ignored all my classes in the last few days, so I should probably try to put in some study time today," Will told her.

"How about we meet on the steps of the Rock in about an hour and a half?"

"Sounds good," Nancy agreed. She needed to go to the Rockhausen Library anyway to do some research for her western civilization class.

A few moments later she hung up the phone and put it quietly on her dresser. Then she started collecting shampoo, toothbrush, and cosmetics bottles. It wasn't until she was grabbing her bathrobe that she saw the blinking light on the answering machine she and Kara shared.

The night before, she'd gotten back so late from the party and was so tired that she hadn't even thought to check her messages. *Please* be Jake, she thought. She hurried back across the room and hit the Play button, turning the volume down low.

"Hi, stranger. Looks like we missed each other . . . again."

Just the sound of Jake's voice, even his recorded voice, made Nancy smile to herself. He sounded as if he missed her as much as she missed him.

"I'll be home all day tomorrow," the message went on. "Any chance I might be able to talk to *you* instead of to this machine?"

"Definitely," Nancy murmured. "Sooner than you think."

Dropping her cosmetics and shampoo into a pile on her bed, she pulled off her nightshirt and found some jeans and a long-sleeved shirt. Racing to the bathroom, she quickly cleaned her face and teeth, and pulled a brush through her reddish blond hair a few times. Back in her room, Nancy put on a pair of boots, grabbed her jacket, bag, and car keys, and flew downstairs and out to the parking lot.

As she pulled up to the curb in front of Jake's apartment house, Nancy looked at her watch. Eight-thirty. It *was* kind of early. Jake and his roommates were bound to be sleeping.

But not for long.

Before Nancy could think about chickening out, she hopped out of the car, strode up the porch stairs, and rang the bell to his second-floor apartment.

"Just a sec!" Jake's voice called out an upstairs window.

He even sounded awake. She heard his footsteps pounding down the stairs, and a second later the front door opened.

"Surprise," Nancy said, grinning at him. "I know it's early, but—"

She broke off when she saw the fuzzy black-and-white creature Jake was holding "A kitten!" she exclaimed. "Where did you get it?"

Jake shot her a lopsided smile. "Four of them, actually. Plus their mother." As he tried to keep the furry thing under control, the look on his face was so hilarious that Nancy broke out laughing.

"What's going on?" she asked him. "Are you opening a home for wayward cats?"

"Explanations will have to wait," he said, holding up a hand. "First . . ."

His brown eyes locked on hers, and Nancy felt that wonderful feeling she always got when he looked at her. "Yes?" she prompted, feeling slightly out of breath.

"First, I want to give you a proper hello." Jake bent toward her, covering her mouth in a long, lingering kiss. "Good morning," he murmured, pulling his lips a fraction of an inch away from hers.

"I'll say," she murmured. "My dad'll be glad to hear that I'm dating a guy with such good manners."

"I hope so," Jake said. Then he jumped back and cried, "Ouch! Those claws hurt."

Nancy laughed as he pulled the kitten from his shirt. "Come on," he told her. "I'll show you his brothers and sisters."

She followed Jake inside and up the stairs to the second-floor landing. As she stepped through his apartment door and into the living room, she saw a full-grown cat curled up in a wicker basket lined with a towel. Her paws were stretched protectively around three other sleeping kittens.

"I've been taking care of these guys since I found them yesterday afternoon," Jake said. He sat down on the couch in his living room, and the kitten immediately started clambering all over him.

"Mama over there was clipped by a car. I found her by the side of the road in town yesterday, with these little guys shivering behind a hydrant a few feet away. I took them to a vet, and he said Mama here was lucky. Only some bad bruises and some cuts."

Nancy sat down next to Jake and reached over to pet the kitten. "The poor things. Are they strays?"

"Yes, I'm pretty sure," Jake answered. "I couldn't just leave them there. The mother hasn't been eating much solid food yet, still a little traumatized probably, so I've been giving her and the kittens milk." He nodded to a plastic baby bottle that lay on the coffee table. "Carly said that if I hadn't taken her when I did, she might have died of shock. And then the kittens wouldn't have had a chance."

"Carly?" Nancy echoed, raising an eyebrow at him.

Jake shot her an amused glance. "She runs the Animal Rescue League here in Weston," he said. "The vet suggested I take the cats there after he examined the mother. Carly is a great lady. Reminds me of my grandmother. Anyway, she had no room for this family, so I offered to help out."

"I can't wait to meet her," Nancy said, grinning. "No wonder you've been so busy. I was beginning to think we wouldn't be able to have another date until next semester."

Jake gave her another one of his irresistible lopsided smiles. "It's only been three days."

"Is that all?" she asked, shooting him a teasing smile.

"Seems like longer, though," Jake conceded. "A lot longer."

He leaned in, covering her mouth in another kiss that seemed to go on forever.

"Ahem!"

Nancy pulled away from Jake, her lips still tingling. She jumped when she realized that two guys were in the living room with her and Jake. One was tall, with brown skin and close-cropped black hair. He was wearing sweats and a T-shirt and had obviously just woken up. The other was about her height, with olive skin, and straight dark hair that was still wet from a shower. Both guys were staring at Nancy with open curiosity.

"Are we interrupting something?" asked the shorter guy, his brown eyes sparkling with mischief.

"You know you are," Jake shot back.

"So she really does exist," the taller guy said, shaking his head in disbelief. "We were beginning to think that Jake made you up. You *are* Nancy Drew, right?"

"In the flesh," Nancy shot back with a grin.

Jake let out a sigh and straightened away from her. "Nancy, meet my housemates. Nick Dimartini and Dennis Larkin. Great timing, guys."

"Hi, housemates," Nancy said amiably.

"Nice to meet you, finally," Dennis said, shaking her hand.

"Ditto," said Nick. He went over to the basket and picked up one of the kittens. "Hey, you're not interested in adopting these things, are you?"

Nancy shook her head. "There's a rule. No pets in the dorms."

"Too bad," Dennis said. "That really limits our choices of where to dump all the animals Jake's been dragging home this week."

"Animals? As in, more than just this one time?" Nancy asked, looking at Jake in surprise.

He gave a shrug. "When I see a creature in need, I do something, that's all."

"Correction. You make us *all* do something," Nick said, rolling his eyes. "We just finished finding a home for that stray dog you found, and then you decide to adopt a family of cats."

"I had no idea," Nancy said, shooting Jake a surprised look.

Again, Jake simply shrugged. "It's not a secret. We've just been so busy, I haven't had a chance to tell you, that's all." He shot her a sideways look, hesitating for a moment. "It doesn't bother you, does it?"

"Are you kidding? I think it's great!" She threw her arms around Jake's neck and planted a kiss on his cheek. "Whoever would have guessed that such a hard-boiled investigative reporter could be such a softie deep down."

"Shhh!" he said in a stage whisper. "You'll ruin my reputation."

"Don't worry," Nancy said. "Your secret is safe with me."

Bess stepped out of the shower in the Kappas' bathroom on Saturday morning. After drying off, she wrapped her wet hair in a towel, then looked down at the overflowing shoulder bag that she'd dropped in the corner. The clothes she'd worn the night before were draped over the bag. She reached beneath them for her makeup case and the travel toothbrush she'd started carrying around recently.

I'm going to have to start carting my whole wardrobe around with me, she thought. Except that soon there might not be *any* place I feel comfortable sleeping.

She wasn't sure why she'd decided to spend the night on the couch here at the sorority. After the ice-cold way Holly had treated her at the movie, she didn't think Holly would appreciate her being around. But sleeping in her own room at Jamison definitely *wasn't* an option. There was no way she could have put up with Leslie yelling at her every time she breathed the wrong way. She probably could have crashed in Nancy's suite, but ...

"You can't just keep running away from what's bothering you," she told her reflection. Even if it was uncomfortable seeing Holly here at Kappa, maybe they'd at least have a chance to talk things out.

Letting out a sigh, Bess brushed out her hair and put on the same clothes she'd worn the night before. Then, stuffing the rest of her things back in her shoulder bag, she tugged the strap over her shoulder and stepped into the upstairs hallway.

She was halfway to the stairs when Holly's door opened right next to her.

"Oh," Holly said, looking surprised. She was wearing her jacket and had a flat portfolio tucked under her arm.

"Hi," Bess said, shooting her a tentative smile. "I was hoping we could talk."

"Oh?" There was a hopeful glimmer in Holly's eyes as she spoke. But then she frowned and added quickly, "Sorry. I don't have time." She closed her bedroom door behind her and started quickly down the stairs, without even giving Bess a second glance. "See you."

Bess heard the front door open downstairs. When it closed again, the *thunk* sounded hollow and empty. "Yeah, right," she said to the empty hallway.

She sat down on the top step and rested her chin on her knees. I can't seem to make *anyone* happy these days.

"Good morning, Bess," a familiar and totally insincere voice spoke up behind her. Looking over her shoulder, Bess saw Soozie walking toward her, wearing a terrycloth robe over her nightgown.

"Hi, Soozie," Bess said, stifling a groan.

"Listen, I'm sorry to hear about you and Holly," Soozie said.

Bess made a vague gesture that she hoped would pass for an answer. The last thing she wanted was for Soozie to get mixed up in this whole thing.

Soozie gave her a disgustingly sweet smile. "I just want you to know that I'm keeping an open mind," she went on. "I'm sure Holly was just letting off some steam when she said those things about you and your friends."

"What are you talking about?" Bess asked before she could stop herself. "Didn't Holly get my note?"

"Sure." Soozie blinked, looking surprised. "I'm sorry. Maybe I misunderstood what she was saying." She patted Bess on the shoulder before heading back down the hall to the bathroom. "Forget I mentioned it."

As if that was possible. Bess couldn't believe that Holly would be so quick to judge her—especially when she had gone out of her way to show Holly that she believed in her. The more Bess thought about it, the angrier she got.

Bess go to her feet. All she wanted to do was get out of there. But before she'd taken more than a step, she got another idea.

Turning around, she went quickly to Holly's door, turned the knob, and went inside. As soon as the door was closed behind her, she dropped her bag to the floor and looked around.

"I can't believe I'm doing this," she whispered aloud. She still didn't think Holly had taken the Cherokee artifacts. But standing up for Holly hadn't done Bess any good. She might as well search her room and get it over with. Then at least she could get Will off her back.

Taking a deep breath, Bess opened Holly's

closet door and began poking into the shoes and boots lined up on the floor.

This is ridiculous, she told herself. You know you're not going to find anything, and—

Suddenly Bess heard something—a noise right outside Holly's door! Oh, no, she thought, standing bolt upright.

Before Bess could move, the door swung open, and Holly stepped in. She started toward her desk, then stopped short when she saw Bess.

"Holly, I . . ." Bess's voice trailed off helplessly. She knew there was no way to talk her way out of this one.

The surprised expression in Holly's eyes hardened to a steely glare. Dropping her portfolio to the ground, she faced Bess and placed her hands squarely on her hips.

"I hope you're not doing what I think you are," she told Bess in an angry voice. "Because if you're snooping around here trying to prove that I stole those things for Will's show, your days as a Kappa pledge are over!"

CHAPTER 11

"Do you think you can stay away from the kittens long enough to get in some study time?" Nancy asked Jake as they left his apartment.

"I don't have a choice," he answered. He balanced toast and a plastic coffee mug in one hand while he reached with the other to open Nancy's passenger door. "I've got a paper due on Tuesday. Besides, if I stay away from campus for too long, I start to feel cut off from what's going on there."

"Not a good sign . . ." Nancy shot him a teasing grin over the top of her car before climbing in behind the wheel. "Especially for a hard-boiled pussycat—I mean, *reporter*—like yourself."

Jake's mouth twisted in something between a grimace and a smile. "All right, all right," he mumbled through a mouthful of toast.

Nancy laughed as she turned the key in the

ignition, then started driving back toward campus. "George and Will are talking to the police this morning to find out if they've had any luck tracking down the artifacts."

Jake and Nancy had discussed the stolen artifacts while feeding the kittens, and Nancy had filled him in on what she learned about Holly at the party the night before.

"I bet they'll be glad to know that Holly couldn't have taken them," Jake put in.

Nancy nodded. She'd left a message on Bess's machine, but she'd forgotten to mention it to Will when he called.

"Definitely," she agreed. "I'm supposed to meet them outside the Rock"—she shot a quick glance at her watch, then grimaced—"ten minutes ago."

"You can blame me," Jake said. "Tell them I forced you at gunpoint to meet my housemates and help feed my cats."

"You're so ruthless," Nancy said.

Nancy drove down Wilder's main road until the huge granite library came into sight. Will and George were sitting at the top of the wide stone steps that led up to the entrance. George's crutches were propped next to her. Nancy leaned on her horn, stopping in the center of the drive. "George!" she yelled as Jake opened his window.

"I think she heard you," Jake said dryly, tugging at his ear. "I think the whole campus heard you."

As first Will, and then George, struggling with

her crutches, came down the stairs toward them, Nancy called out, "I have to park the car. We'll be there as soon as we—"

A car horn blared right behind the Mustang.

"Uh-oh, traffic jam," Jake murmured, glancing over his shoulder.

Looking in her rearview mirror, Nancy saw that a yellow rental van was right behind her. The driver was gesturing anxiously for her to move, signaling with his blinker to pass.

"That's Seth Klein," Will said as he and George came up to the passenger window of Nancy's car as she was pulling over to the curb. He waved at the van and called, "Seth!"

"Who's Seth Klein?" Jake wanted to know.

Nancy got a glimpse of blow-dried brown hair and an impatient, tanned face. Seth was in such a hurry to pass her that he barely seemed to notice Will. He gave a distracted wave. As soon as Nancy pulled over, Seth shot past her car.

"What's his problem?" George asked, staring after the rental van.

"Who's Seth?" Jake asked again, but Nancy was so preoccupied that she barely heard him.

"Why is he in such a hurry?" she wondered aloud. "Maybe I'm just being paranoid, but—"

"Let's follow him," Will said.

Jake opened his mouth, then shut it again and got out, climbing into the backseat with Will. As George maneuvered her crutches into the front, Nancy started after the van.

"We didn't learn much at the police station,"

George said, turning to Nancy with a sober look. "The detectives who went to the Borrosian Gallery struck out. The owner wasn't there, and his assistant wouldn't talk to—"

She broke off as Jake let out a loud, piercing whistle. "Will someone *please* tell me who Seth Klein is!" he cried into the silence that followed.

Nancy shot him an apologetic smile before pulling her attention back to the van up ahead. "Sorry, we'll explain everything while we drive, Jake."

Bess had never felt so humiliated in her entire life. Somehow, she had to try to straighten this mess out.

But how?

"I don't think you stole anything,", she told Holly. "I've been *defending* you to Will."

"Oh, really?" Holly shot her a look of disbelief that cut Bess to the bone. "Then what are you doing here?"

"I thought . . . I thought I would at least help prove to will that you *didn't* take the artifacts . . . by checking your room." Bess stumbled over her words, blinking back hot tears. "I wouldn't have done it, but you were so cold to me, even after I left you the—"

"Why *wouldn't* I be cold?" Holly interrupted angrily. "I heard about what you told Eileen and Casey about me."

Bess blinked in confusion. "Eileen and Casey? What are you talking about?" she asked. She hadn't said a word to either of them about Holly *or* the stolen artifacts.

"Don't play innocent," Holly scoffed, her voice rising. "I thought we were friends. Then suddenly I hear that you're telling people that it's just a matter of time before the police prove that *I* stole that stuff from Will's tribe."

"I'd never do something like that!" Bess said hotly. Her mind was spinning. How could Holly accuse her of being so mean? *"You're* the one spreading rumors!" she shot back. "I went out of my way to show you that I believed you. I didn't have to leave you that note."

"Note?" Holly echoed, but Bess wasn't going to let her interrupt.

"I didn't have to stick up for you," Bess yelled. "And right now I wish I hadn't, since all you did was turn around and bad-mouth me to everyone here. If that's the way you treat your *friends,* then I guess Kappa's not for me after all!"

Bess was so angry and upset that she couldn't even see straight. She stumbled blindly toward Holly's door. Suddenly she had to get out of there.

"Bess, wait!"

Bess stopped with her hand on the doorknob. She had to take a few deep breaths before she could turn around and look at Holly. When she did, she saw that Holly's hands had dropped to her sides and the anger had totally left her face. "You left me a note?" she asked.

"Didn't you get it?" Bess asked. She was feeling more confused than ever. "Soozie said that—"

"Soozie?" Holly interrupted. She stared out into the hallway, frowning. For the first time, Bess realized that a few of the sorority sisters were standing outside Holly's door, looking concerned. Holly gave them a preoccupied glance before closing the door and turning back to Bess. "Why didn't I think of it before?" she murmured.

Suddenly things were starting to make more sense to Bess. "You *didn't* get the note," she said. "But Soozie made it sound as if you did."

"She must have taken it before I could read it," Holly said, nodding. "She's the one who told me that you said that stuff to Casey and Eileen."

"She's been lying to both of us," Bess said, "trying to set us against each other."

"You know how much Soozie and I *don't* get along. She would do anything to make sure that anyone I'm friends with quits Kappa."

"The worst part is, it almost worked," Bess said sadly.

Holly shook her head slowly back and forth. "I don't know why I believed her. I was so busy trying to get everything together in case the jury committee decides to mount my show. Then I guess I felt hurt because it seemed like you were taking Will's side. And when I saw you in here . . ."

Bess saw the moody glimmer return to Holly's eyes. "I'm sorry," Bess said quickly. "I know there's no excuse for sneaking in here. I was just so desperate."

"Well"—Holly gave Bess a weak smile, then reached over to hug her—"I guess it's partly my fault. I should have had more faith in you."

Bess felt as if the clouds had parted after a terrible thunderstorm, revealing a clear blue sky. "I'm just glad we can be friends again," she said, grinning.

"Let's get some breakfast," Holly said. "I was going to head over to Kaplan, but now I think I'll stick around here long enough to talk to Soozie."

"Definitely," Bess agreed.

As the two of them headed downstairs, the front door opened and Eileen came in. "Anyone want to head over to today's football game?" she asked, plunking down her sketch pad in the foyer. "Pregame show's at eleven-thirty."

Bess shot Holly a hopeful look.

"I wanted to talk to Soozie. And I *should* get over to Kaplan," Holly said, shaking her head. "I have to go over designs for my announcements, and—"

"Fifth row, right on the fifty-yard line," Eileen said, holding up a handful of tickets. "My dad's an alum with season tickets, and he couldn't use them."

"We'll just stay for the first half," Bess begged Holly. "Then I'll come back and help you. I promise."

Holly smiled, putting her arm through Bess's. "I guess I can take a few hours off," she conceded. "Let's go!"

* * *

Paul Cody closed and sealed the envelope, then pulled a pen from his desk drawer and wrote Bess's name on it. It had taken him all morning, but he'd finally come up with a plan to cheer her up. After the way last night ended, he figured that she could use it.

"What's that smell?" Emmet Lehman sniffed the air, picking his way around the mountain of dirty socks, shirts, and pants that Paul had dumped in the middle of their room. "Gee, Paul, you didn't have to clean up just for me," he said sarcastically.

"I got caught up," Paul told him. "Anyway, don't you have to be somewhere? Like, at Holliston Stadium? You guys are playing today, right?"

"Oh, gee. Are we?" Emmet asked, scratching his head and shooting Paul an exaggerated moronic look. "Don't ask me. I'm just a brainless jock."

"Who happens to be a chem major," Paul added, shaking his head. "I tried to look at one of your books once. I couldn't even figure out which way was up."

Emmet laughed, heading for his closet to grab his sports bag. "Maybe you'd better stick to watching football instead of science books. Kickoff's in an hour and a half."

As Emmet shoved some things into his bag, Paul noticed him shoot a glance at the envelope addressed to Bess on Paul's desk. "Last night go well?"

"Everything went great, actually. Right up until Bess almost started crying."

"Nice effect you have on women," Emmet said, laughing.

"It wasn't my fault," Paul insisted.

"I see," Emmet said doubtfully.

Paul still wasn't too clear on what exactly had been so upsetting. Bess had said she was too bummed out to talk about it, and he hadn't wanted to pry. But it was obvious that she was having some kind of fight with some of her friends.

He'd spent the rest of the evening making dumb jokes, but she still seemed depressed when he dropped her off at Kappa house.

"Anyway, whatever's bothering her, I think I came up with a way to make her forget about it," Paul said. "I *can* be pretty creative, you know." He ignored the look of disbelief Emmet shot him. "Now help me find a pledge. I need someone to make a special delivery to Kappa House later."

Nancy leaned forward over the driver's wheel and peered through the windshield of her Mustang. Seth's yellow rental van was just visible several car lengths ahead, moving slowly through Chicago's clogged downtown area.

"I wonder why he came all the way to Chicago?" George spoke up from the passenger seat. "You don't think he's going to the airport, do you?"

Nancy shook her head. "We saw signs for the airport south of the main part of the city. He wouldn't have bothered to come all the way here."

Glancing in the rearview mirror, she saw that Will was scouring the buildings on either side of them. "Looks like there are a lot of galleries around here," he said. "Maybe he's going to the Borrosian."

"The place that's interested in buying Cherokee crafts?" Jake asked.

"Yes," George answered. "The cops weren't able to talk to Erik Borrosian, the owner. Maybe he and Seth Klein *do* have some kind of deal brewing."

"He's pulling over," Nancy broke in.

The van was stopping next to a fire hydrant, about half a dozen car lengths ahead. "You guys, we're never going to find a spot."

"Never say never," George spoke up with a grin. She flicked a thumb toward a sedan that was pulling away from a meter just in front of them. "Looks like it's our lucky day. And check out where Seth Klein is going."

Nancy caught a glimpse of a fancy-looking gallery with a large tribal mask in the window. "Borrosian Gallery," she said, reading the sign over the window. She quickly angled into the parking spot that had just been vacated, then she, George, Jake, and Will all piled out of the car.

"The police said to stay out of it, but I'm not going to sit back and watch while Seth Klein sells my tribe's heritage." Will's jaw went tight, and he walked quickly toward the gallery.

Nancy caught the anxious look on George's face as she swung after him on her crutches. The two girls and Jake reached the gallery door a few steps behind Will.

Throwing a quick glance around, Nancy saw wooden masks and sculptures arranged around the immaculate, airy room. Seth Klein stood next to a desk against the right wall. He was opening up his briefcase while talking to a tall man with balding blond hair. His smooth, easygoing expression changed to surprise when he saw Will, Nancy, Jake, and George.

"Hi," Seth said. "What are you doing here?"

"Never mind about us," Will tossed back, glowering. "What are *you* doing here?"

Seth frowned. "What's going on, Will? I've got business to take care of."

"I'll bet." Will's voice had risen.

The balding man stepped forward, shooting Will a disapproving look. "You've got a lot of nerve barging into my gallery this way."

"It's okay, Erik. I'll take care of it," Seth said quickly. Turning back to Will, he said, "What, exactly, do you *think* I'm doing here?"

Seth seemed genuinely perplexed, thought Nancy. Not at all as if he'd been caught selling stolen artifacts on the black market. "Uh, Will?" she said softly. "Can I speak to you for a minute?"

"You were just waiting for the chance to take

the Cherokee artifacts," Will told Seth, ignoring Nancy. "I heard what you said about how you'd love to make the kind of money the artifacts would bring."

Seth's mouth fell open. "You actually think I'd steal them?"

Nancy caught the unsure looks that George and Jake both shot her. Uh-oh. She was beginning to get the feeling that they'd made a big mistake. "What *are* you doing here?" she asked Seth.

Seth looked at her blankly, then brushed an annoyed hand through his thick hair. "Do I know you?"

"This is Nancy Drew," George spoke up. "She's been helping us try to find out who took the artifacts."

"And I'm Jake Collins," Jake added.

Seth's angry eyes flitted over all of them, then settled on Will. "If I didn't have deep respect for Dan Chekelelee, I'd call the cops right now and have you four thrown out of here."

Nancy, Will, George, and Jake all looked at one another uncertainly.

"You want to know why I'm here?" Seth went on curtly. "Fine. I'll tell you. Mr. Borrosian is interested in purchasing some Cherokee crafts, and I happen to represent several talented artisans from the Cherokee Nation." He took a plastic sheet from his briefcase that had several slides in it. "I brought him slides of some pieces I thought he might like."

There was an uncertain set to Will's strong features as he took the sheet of slides and looked at them. "These aren't the artifacts that were stolen," he confirmed.

That didn't necessarily mean that Seth *didn't* take the older, more valuable artifacts, thought Nancy. But her gut feeling was that he wasn't involved in the theft.

"Why didn't you just tell Will that you were doing business with Mr. Borrosian?" she asked. "Why keep it a secret?"

"Just because I didn't talk about it doesn't mean I was keeping it a secret," he said. He must have seen doubt in their eyes, because he quickly added, "What do you want to do? Send in a SWAT team to search my van?"

Nancy saw the uncomfortable glimmer that came into Will's eyes. And the disappointment.

She had to admit, it was frustrating to come all the way here only to run into a dead end.

Now what were they going to do?

CHAPTER 12

George shot Will a sideways glance as they walked down the sidewalk away from the Borrosian Gallery. She tried to look at the bright side of what had just happened. If she could only think of what the bright side was.

"At least now we know that Seth isn't trying to cheat the Cherokee Nation out of their tribal belongings," she said.

"And, hey, if we made total fools of ourselves while we were at it, then I guess it was worth it," Will added, shooting a rueful grimace at the others. "Right?"

"I'll pass on answering that question, if you don't mind," Jake said.

Will shook his head and let out a groan. "Seth is probably going to tell Dan Chekelelee all about what happened. I can't believe I made such an idiot of myself."

"We *all* charged in," Nancy reminded him.

Will let out another groan. "I don't know about you guys, but after what happened in there, I need to clear my head," he said.

"Distraction. That's what we all need," Jake decided. "Since we're in the big city, how about some lunch? And speaking of distraction . . ." He stopped in front of another gallery, several store-fronts down from the Borrosian. A huge, abstract painting filled the front window. He cocked his head to one side to look at the painting. "Staring at this thing for a while would make anyone's mind go blank."

George laughed, taking in the multicolored swirls. "Or at least make you too dizzy to think about anything else," she said. "Let's take a look inside. As long as we're here, we might as well see what's at the cutting edge of the art world."

Will shrugged. "I don't care. I'm just following you guys. No more decisions today for me."

As they stepped inside, George spotted a man and a woman at the rear of the gallery, talking.

"It's about the dehumanization of mankind," the man was saying as he gestured to a metal sculpture.

George tuned out the rest of what he said. She preferred to make up her own mind about what the work was about. She turned to another piece, made of wide strips of unpainted canvas that hung from the ceiling.

"Looks like someone left their laundry out to

dry," Will whispered, coming up next to her with Nancy and Jake.

"Shhh!" George whispered, jabbing him in the ribs with her elbow. "They'll hear you!"

"I wonder how much it costs," Jake said. He went over to the small plaque that was affixed to the wall behind the piece, then let out a low whistle. "Fourteen thousand dollars!"

Nancy's mouth dropped open. Then she grinned at Jake and punched him gently on the arm. "With that kind of money, you could keep every homeless cat in Weston in cat chow for years."

She was obviously teasing him about something. Before George could ask what it was, the woman at the back of the gallery spoke up.

"It's an exciting time for alternative art," she said. "New talent coming on the scene all the time from the local colleges and universities."

"Have you heard about Wilder University's World of Art series?" the man asked.

That caught George's attention.

"The university's been holding off announcing the premiere show," the man went on, "but I was told by one of the exhibiting students that it's going to be a show of alternative art and design by Wilder students."

George caught the surprised look that Will shot her. He looked grimly over his shoulder at the man and woman, his jaw tight.

"I thought the jury committee was going to

wait a little longer before making a final decision," George whispered.

"They didn't say anything to you about Holly's show definitely being chosen, did they?" Nancy asked. When he shook his head, she said, "Kind of makes you wonder, doesn't it? How did someone else know that Holly's show will go up before the jury committee even decides?"

Jake's brows shot up, forming a line over his eyes. "Unless that person took the Cherokee artifacts, to make sure that Will's show can't be mounted."

George saw the excited look on Nancy's face as she walked over to the man and woman, with Will right beside her. "Excuse me," Nancy said. "I couldn't help overhearing what you just said."

The man stopped talking and gave her a slick, professional smile. "Yes?"

"My friends and I are students at Wilder," Nancy explained. "We know some of the people who might be exhibiting in the alternative art show. We were wondering if maybe we know the person who told you about the show."

The man stared at the wall, his brow furrowed in concentration. After a few moments he shook his head and said, "Sorry. I'm drawing a blank."

George could see the disappointment on Will's face. But Nancy looked as if she were thinking something over.

"Was his name Olson?" Nancy asked. "B. J. Olson?"

"Yes!" the gallery owner snapped his fingers

and nodded. "Now that you mention it, his name *was* Olson."

George exchanged a blank look with Will and Jake. "B. J. Olson?" she whispered, when Nancy and Will came back. "Who's he?"

"One of the students who would be exhibiting in Holly's show," Nancy explained. "I didn't think that it would be worth checking out every single student. I mean, how much attention could any one artist get?"

"But if Chicago galleries are interested in the World of Art series, then it *could* be important to B.J.'s career," Jake finished.

Nancy nodded. "Plus, I happened to find out last night that B.J. was in Kaplan when the artifacts were taken," she said. "Let's head back to Wilder, you guys. We've got to talk to Holly about this."

Bess threw up her hands and cheered along with the thousands of other fans who filled Holliston Stadium. The football players were just filing off the field, and the band struck up the first notes of their half-time show.

"Way to go, Norsemen!" Eileen yelled. She turned to Bess and Holly with a flushed, smiling face. "Twenty-one to zip," she said. "It's a total rout!"

"Too bad I have to miss the second half," Holly said. She checked her watch, then looked at Bess. "You don't have to come. I'll be all right on my own."

"I don't mind," Bess said. "Wilder is so far ahead that the second half will probably be a snore."

Eileen grinned up at them. "I'll let you know," she said. "I'm going to stick it out a little while longer. See you, guys!"

Bess and Holly wound their way through the stadium to the exit. Bess stopped when she saw a pay phone just outside the stadium. "I want to call into my machine," she told Holly. "I haven't been to my dorm since yesterday."

"Busy with Paul?" Holly guessed. "You looked pretty cozy when I saw you last night."

Bess grinned. It felt great to know that things between her and Holly were back to normal. "I've been kind of distracted lately," she told Holly, "but I don't think he's given up on me yet."

"If you ask me, it would take a nuclear explosion to make him give up on you," Holly laughed.

"Yeah, well . . ."

Bess put some change in the slot, dialed her number, and punched in her code when the beep sounded. After listening to her messages, she hung up and turned to Holly with a grin.

"Nancy called this morning. She said she found out that you couldn't have stolen the Cherokee artifacts," she said in a rush. "Now Will *has* to get off my case."

Holly just rolled her eyes. "And mine," she added. "Finally."

"I guess that makes Frank Chung the most likely person to have taken them," Bess said, thinking out loud.

"Um, Bess? Can we *please* talk about something besides the artifacts?" Holly asked. "Those things have already caused enough trouble between us."

Bess clamped her mouth shut. "Right," she said. "By the way, did I tell you that Casey and I are going to audition for the Drama Club's one-act plays?"

Nancy angled her car down Wilder University's twisting drives, heading for Sorority Row. "I hope Holly's at Kappa House," she said. "If not, we'll head over to Kaplan."

"Hold up a sec, Nancy," George said from the passenger seat. "Isn't that Frank Chung?"

Nancy's gaze flitted to the left, where George was looking. "It *is* him," she realized. He was standing outside a white Victorian house, spray-painting a huge sheet of poster board.

"Spray paint," Jake said. "Didn't you say—"

"That someone spray-painted the security camera in the store room when the artifacts were taken?" Will finished.

"Someone did," Nancy confirmed. "Plus, I saw red spray paint *and* that weird blue-and-black fabric in Frank Chung's bag yesterday."

Glancing in the rearview mirror, Nancy saw Will's mouth settle into a determined line. "I still say we need to find out about B.J. But as long as we're here, we might as well stop," he said.

"Let's go easy on the questions this time," Nancy advised as she pulled over to the curb. "Remember what happened at the Borrosian Gallery."

Will grimaced. "Don't remind me," he said. "We'll be subtle, I promise."

"I'll wait here," Jake said.

"Me, too," George added. "We don't want the guy to get too defensive."

Frank shot Nancy and Will a curious look as they walked up the driveway toward him. "Hi," he said. "What's up?"

"Well, actually . . ." Nancy looked at the can of red spray-paint in his hand. Then her gaze moved to a crumpled-up shirt that lay in a pile next to the poster board and another can of paint. The shirt was made of the same blue-and-black fabric she'd seen in Frank's bag the night before.

"We were just wondering where you got that," Will said, frowning.

Frank's eyes looked slightly nervous. "I took it from the art center," he finally said. "But I'm an art major, and I didn't think it was any big deal to borrow some paint from the department. Anyway, I found the can by the garbage. If it's yours, why don't you just say so? I'll give it back or get you a new can."

"You found it in the garbage?" Nancy echoed.

Frank nodded. "I need to make some posters

for the Asian Society," he said, gesturing toward the white house behind him. "I figured it was only a can of paint."

"What about that shirt?" Will cut in.

"The can was wrapped in it. There wasn't any top, so I just took the whole thing." Frank shot Will a dubious look. "Don't tell me you want *that* back, too?"

As Frank talked, Nancy had a hard time picturing him as a scheming thief. "Could you just tell us *when* you found the stuff?" she asked.

Frank shrugged. "Yesterday morning, around eight-thirty. I was going to see if I could get the Art Department to donate paint. Then I found this."

"Thanks," Nancy told him.

She and Will practically ran back to her Mustang. "It all fits," she said as she got back in behind the wheel. "If B.J. stole the artifacts, it makes sense that he'd get rid of the paint."

"And the shirt, once he found out that it was ripped," Will added.

Nancy turned the key in the ignition, and looked at the others. "Next stop, Kappa House!"

"So, we're down to two choices now, right?" Bess asked Holly.

"Yes," Holly answered. She slipped a slide into the small viewer in her hand, then passed it to Bess. "Here's the first one."

They were sitting on the couch in the Kappa living room. On the table in front of them was the announcement Holly had designed. A huge space at the center was reserved for a photograph of one of the student works. All they had to do was choose which piece would be featured.

Bess was just lifting the viewer to her eyes when the doorbell rang. Seconds later someone answered it, and Bess heard Nancy's voice: "Is Holly around?"

"In here!" Holly called.

Nancy wasn't alone, Bess saw. Will and Jake came into the living room with her, followed by George, on her crutches. Seeing the serious looks on their faces, Bess felt her stomach tighten.

"I got your message, Nancy," Bess said. "What's up, you guys?"

"There's no easy way to say this," Nancy began. "We think that B. J. Olson might be the person who stole the Cherokee artifacts."

Bess didn't notice the slight frown that darkened Holly's brow. "B.J. would never do anything so insane," she said quietly. "What makes you think it's him?"

Bess sat motionless on the couch. *Just when I thought everything was all right. Please, don't let this turn into a screaming match,* she begged silently.

She and Holly both listened while Nancy went through her list of reasons. When she was done, Bess had to admit that it could have been him.

"He's contacting galleries?" she asked Holly. "Before the jury committee even makes their final decision about your show going up?"

For a moment Holly sat there frowning. Finally she turned to Will and asked, "What do you want me to do?"

Just then the Kappas' front door banged open. "I couldn't take watching the game anymore," Eileen called out. "It was too pathetic. Thirty to nothing when I left."

She came into the living room, carrying her jumbo sketch pad, then stopped when she saw everyone. "Hi! Listen, don't mind me," Eileen said quickly. "I just need a big enough space to look at all the sketches I've done so far. I'll be quiet as a mouse."

Bess caught the concerned expression on Will's face. "We're kind of in the middle of something important," she began.

But she could see that it was already too late. Two more Kappa sisters appeared from upstairs. As soon as they saw Eileen tacking up the drawings, they came in to take a look.

"Oh, my gosh!" a sorority sister cried, staring at one of the sketches. "I look awful!"

Another girl started laughing. "At least you're wearing clothes," she said. "Look at me, I've got my bathrobe on."

"Um, could we talk upstairs, Holly?" Will asked. But Bess couldn't help taking a minute to look at the drawings. Even George and Jake were getting in on the action.

"Hey, Nancy," Jake said. "Everyone in your suite has been immortalized."

He flicked a thumb at a drawing of Reva,

Ginny, Stephanie, and Kara, but Bess noticed Nancy didn't seem to see it or even hear Jake. Instead, she was gazing at a sketch that looked as if it had been done in an art studio.

Bess stepped closer to the sketch. She didn't see anything special about it. The two figures were well done—Bess recognized Holly right away but couldn't figure out who the guy with wiry hair and glasses was. So why was Nancy so interested in it? She wouldn't stop staring at the picture.

"That's B. J. Olson, isn't it?" Nancy suddenly asked Eileen, her eyes still on the drawing.

"Yes," Eileen answered. "Along with the sculpture he swears is going to make him famous. Apparently, he's already got a gallery interested."

Bess noticed that this piece of information seemed to really get Nancy's attention. "Oh?" Nancy commented.

As Bess watched, Nancy shifted her gaze to the tangle of video screens, wires, and metal that Eileen had sketched behind the figures. "I saw that piece yesterday, but it looks different in the drawing," Nancy said. "I don't know, smaller or something."

"It *was* smaller," Holly spoke up. "Just when I thought B.J. was done, he changed his mind and decided to add a row of about half a dozen new video screens." She ran her finger along the left of the drawing of the sculpture. "Right there."

"Half a dozen, huh?" Nancy stared at the drawing again before turning to Eileen. "When did you do that drawing?" she asked. "Before Friday morning?"

"Let's see . . . Well, yes, as a matter of fact, it was Wednesday afternoon, right?' Eileen said, looking at Holly. "Before we went to find out—"

"That my proposal didn't get chosen for the World of Art exhibit," Holly finished glumly.

Bess thought she would scream if Nancy didn't let on soon to what she was thinking. She knew that pensive look her friend got. Then Nancy's expression changed from one of thoughtfulness to barely contained excitement. Bess couldn't stand it anymore. "Nancy, what is it?"

"You guys," Nancy said, looking around at everyone. "I'm pretty sure I know where the Cherokee artifacts are. They've been right under our noses the whole time!"

Chapter 13

W hat!" everyone cried at once.

The more she reasoned it out, the more it made sense, Nancy thought. Out loud she said, "Think about it: The artifacts were taken from the storeroom early yesterday morning. The security tape didn't show anyone leaving Kaplan with any kind of bundle that could be the artifacts, so it makes sense that they were still inside the building. Then, when I saw B.J. in his studio late the same afternoon, his sculpture was suddenly larger by *six* video screens."

"Which happens to be almost the exact number of artifacts that were stolen!" Will finished. Nancy could practically see the light blink on inside his head. "Even though seven pieces were taken, a couple of them weren't that big. They could have been stored together inside one screen."

"I don't believe it. So the artifacts *haven't* been sold. They're not gone for good." George pivoted around to grin at Will. "This is great!"

"We haven't recovered them yet," Nancy warned. "This is all speculation. B.J. could also have nothing inside those video screens."

Will had already starting toward the Kappas' front door. "I still think we should head over to Kaplan right away."

Nancy saw the distressed expression on Holly's face. "B.J. *was* talking about a gallery in Chicago being impressed that he might be in the premiere World of Art exhibit," Holly said slowly. "But I still can't believe he's the criminal type."

"What about the scrap of fabric that I mentioned when I saw you yesterday?" Nancy asked. "I got the feeling that you recognized the description."

"I've seen it, but I'm not sure where. I guess it *could* have been in B.J.'s studio," Holly told her. "I'd hate to think . . ."

Bess shot a sympathetic glance at Holly. "We don't *all* have to go over to Kaplan, do we?" she asked Nancy. "Holly and I might as well stay here."

Bess obviously wanted to spare Holly the pain of being on the scene if it turned out that B.J. did have the stolen artifacts. Eileen seemed to pick up on the same thought, because she said, "I'll stick around, too. I still want to find out what everyone thinks of these drawings."

"And I really do have to get over to the Rock to study," Jake added.

Nancy nodded, then turned to George and Will. "Ready?"

"Those earrings look incredible on you," Ray said as he and Ginny stepped into her room at Thayer Hall. "Turquoise and silver suit you."

"I agree." Ginny tossed her room key on her dresser, then bounced down on her bed. "In case I haven't already told you enough, I love the earrings, Ray." She smiled shyly up at him.

"I know, I know, stop thanking me," Ray murmured. Sitting next to her on the bed, he slipped an arm around Ginny's waist and kissed her on the mouth. She held on to him, pressing harder and harder, losing herself in his intense heat.

"Phone," he whispered, pulling back the slightest bit.

It took her a second to realize that the phone on her desk was ringing and ringing. Letting out a groan, she got up to answer it. "Hello?"

"Hello, Ginny."

"Mother! What a surprise." Ginny shot a look at Ray and shrugged helplessly. "How's everything?"

"We're all just fine," her mother told her. "I've got great news."

Ray came up behind her and kissed her gently on the back of the neck, sending a shiver up and down her spine. "Oh, yeah?" she said into the receiver.

"Are you all right?" her mother asked, sounding suddenly concerned. "Your voice sounds strange. Are you getting a cold?"

Ginny twisted firmly away from Ray, glaring at him. "I'm fine, Mother. What's the great news?"

"Well, your father, sister, and I can finally get away from everything here for a few days," Mrs. Yuen announced. "We're coming to visit!"

Ginny's breath caught in her throat. She had to swallow a few times before she could say anything. "That's, uh, great. I can't wait," she said, trying to sound excited.

But deep down she was anything but thrilled. She shot a quick look at Ray, and panic welled up inside of her as she imagined him in the same room as her parents.

Ray, meet my mom and dad, the most conservative, traditional people on the planet. Mother? Father? This is my rocker boyfriend. Like his earring?

Oh, my gosh, she thought. This is going to be a disaster!

"Where's B.J.'s studio?" Will asked as he emerged from the stairway onto the fourth floor of the Kaplan Center for the Arts. Nancy and George followed him.

"It's about the middle of the hall," Nancy said. She started down the paint-splattered, industrial-looking hallway, glancing into each studio she passed. "I don't know if he'll even be there, but—"

She broke off as her eyes fell on B.J.'s wiry figure inside one of the studios. He was standing with his back to her, in front of his mixed-media sculpture, applying some kind of strong-smelling finish. Nancy's eyes immediately fell on the six video screens that ran in a vertical line at one side of the sculpture.

"Hi, B.J.," she said, stopping just outside the studio door.

He turned around and looked at her blankly for a moment, then snapped his fingers and grinned. "Nancy Drew, right?"

"Good memory." Nancy gestured toward George and Will, who'd come up next to her. "I don't know if you've met my friends, George Fayne and Will Blackfeather."

B.J.'s easy smile faltered the slightest bit when he looked at Will. "Hi," he said. "Is there something I can do for you?"

"You bet there is," Will told him. He strode into the studio, but Nancy spoke up before he could say anything more.

"We heard from Holly that you might be showing in a gallery in Chicago soon," she said quickly. She didn't want to put B.J. on the defensive—at least, not yet. "Congratulations."

"Yeah. That's great news," George added, leaning against the doorway.

B.J. seemed to relax a little. "Thanks," he said, but he still looked confused. It was obvious he was wondering why they were there.

"This thing is pretty amazing," Will commented, stepping over to B.J.'s sculpture. "Looks like you've got everything in here but the kitchen sink."

"Yeah, well . . ." B.J. said, shooting Will a nervous smile, "I like to work with unusual materials."

"How about *stolen* materials," Will shot back. "Do you like to use those, too?" He reached around to the back of one of the video screens in the vertical row and tried to pry it open.

"Hey! What are you doing?" B.J. cried. "You can't mess with that. That's my work!"

He pulled Will away from the video screen, but Nancy jumped to take his place. Spotting a screwdriver on a cluttered worktable in the corner, she grabbed it and went to work on the small screws that held the back of the screen on.

It took her a few minutes, but finally she was able to lift the back of the video shell off. Inside was a wooden pipe ornamented with feathers, porcupine quills, and shells. "Bingo," she breathed.

She was so entranced by the pipe that it took her a moment to remember why they were there.

"You snake!" Will burst out. Wrenching himself free of B.J.'s grasp, he hauled off and punched him in the jaw, knocking him to the floor. As a stunned B.J. lay there nursing his rapidly swelling lip, Will hurried over to the sculpture and gently lifted out the peace pipe. He and Nancy went to work on the five other video screens.

B.J. groaned. "I can't believe this is happening."

Nancy didn't bother to answer him. She and Will took turns opening the remaining video screens. Ten minutes later an amazing collection of artifacts was lined up on B.J.'s worktable. A soapstone figure, a wooden mask, a beaded bag and moccasins, a woven basket, buckskin robe. As Nancy pulled an old clay pot from the last hollow video casing, B.J. buried his head in his hands. "I knew it was a stupid idea," he mumbled.

"You got *that* right," Will said angrily. He bent over the artifacts, looking them over carefully. "You'd better not have damaged any of these. You're in big enough trouble already, pal."

"I was careful. You have to understand. My whole career could take off after the World of Art show," B.J. said weakly.

George just stared at him, outraged. "You think that justifies stealing artifacts that the Cherokee could never replace?" When B.J. didn't say anything, she shook her head in disgust. "That's really twisted."

"I'm sorry," B.J. finally said. "It's not like I was going to keep the stuff. I was planning to give everything back after Holly's show."

He made it sound as if that made what he'd done all right, but Nancy wasn't about to let him off the hook so easily. "How could you be so sure that Holly's show, and not Frank Chung's, would be chosen to replace Will's?" she asked him.

"My graduate adviser is on the jury committee," B.J. answered. "After Will's show was chosen, he told me that the committee had almost chosen Holly's alternative art proposal. At the last minute they changed their minds and went with the Cherokee artifacts."

"The buzz around campus backed that up," George put in.

"I didn't exactly plan to steal the artifacts," B.J. went on. "But I was here really early on Friday to work on my piece. I saw the guard leave the gallery, and I figured it would take him a while to make the tour of the rest of the building."

"So you decided to make sure Will's show couldn't go on by stealing the artifacts," George finished.

B.J. nodded sheepishly. "The locks on those doors are kind of a joke. All I needed to get in was a credit card and that screwdriver," he explained, nodding to the tool that Nancy had used on the video screens. "I have tons of spray paint. It was easy to paint over the security camera. Ten minutes later the artifacts were hidden in my studio. Luckily, I had extra video screens around," he added. "Sometimes it pays to be a pack rat and a scavenger."

Will looked as if he wanted to punch the guy again, so Nancy stepped smoothly between them.

"You ripped your shirt on one of the hooks in the storeroom, didn't you?" she asked B.J.

"Yeah," B.J. answered, nodding. "I felt it catch, but I didn't realize that a whole piece had ripped off until after I had all the artifacts back here. I figured I'd better ditch the shirt and the paint, just to be safe," he explained. "I tossed them into a pile of stuff next to the trash, by the stairs."

"Where Frank Chung found them," George said, shaking her head in amazement.

"Anyway, what's really important is that you have the stuff back." B.J. turned to Will with an apologetic look on his face. "Right?"

Will just shook his head. "Excuse me if I have a hard time buying your sincere act," he said. "Now that we've found the artifacts, what's *really* important to me is calling the Weston Police Department so they can haul you out of here!"

"So B.J. really did steal the artifacts," Holly said to Bess and Eileen late Saturday afternoon. While Bess and Eileen removed Eileen's sketches from the wall, Holly sat back against the Kappas' living room couch and stared blankly at the coffee table. "I feel awful."

"Why should *you* feel bad?" Eileen asked, putting a handful of sketches in a pile on top of her pad.

"It's not as though you did anything wrong," Bess added. She untacked the last sketch and handed it to Eileen. "B.J. took those artifacts, not you."

A few minutes earlier Nancy had called to tell them that she, George, and Will had found the stolen Cherokee artifacts right where Nancy had guessed they'd be—hidden inside B.J.'s sculpture. Bess was happy the things had been recovered, but she felt sorry for Holly. It had to be a shock to find out that a friend was responsible.

"I know I didn't commit a crime," Holly said slowly. "But knowing he stole those artifacts just to make sure that *my* show would be mounted gives me the creeps." She shook herself, then gave Bess a weak smile. "At least Will got everything back. That's what's important."

"I guess." Bess picked up her overflowing bag from the coffee table and hoisted the strap onto her shoulder. "Well, I guess I should put in an appearance in my dorm. I really need to change," she said, plucking at her sweater.

"I could use a shower myself," Holly said. She leaned forward and looked down at the slides and announcement design that she and Bess had been going over earlier. Scooping it all into a pile, she added, "I guess I won't be needing these anymore."

"Yes, you will," Eileen insisted. She grinned at Holly as she tucked her pad under her arm. "You'll need them for *next* semester's World of Art show."

"Definitely," Bess added with a nod.

Holly didn't exactly jump for joy, but Bess saw

her face brighten a little. "I knew there was a reason I liked you two," Holly said, shaking her head. "You're both hopeless optimists."

When Bess opened the front door a few moments later, she found herself face-to-face with a young man who was carrying an envelope. He looked vaguely familiar, but she couldn't remember where she'd seen him before. "Oh—hello."

"Hello, yourself," he said amiably. "You don't happen to know Bess Marvin, do you? I've got something for her."

Bess looked at the guy in surprise. Who would know to track her down here at the sorority, instead of at her dorm? "I'm Bess."

"Lucky Paul," he murmured. He held out the envelope to her, his dark eyes sparkling with appreciation. "Here you go. Special delivery." Then he tipped an imaginary hat to her, turned around, and jogged back toward the mall.

Just hearing Paul's name made Bess's heart give a little jump. "Thanks!" she called after the guy.

After closing the sorority door behind her, she sat down on the front step. The words "For Bess" were scrawled across the envelope in Paul's handwriting. Beneath them he'd written, "Extremely Urgent—Open Right Away!"

"If you say so," she murmured.

Her whole body tingled with anticipation as she ripped open the envelope and plucked out a small index card. It had just two short sentences on it:

"Find a place where North is South.
Your prize awaits in a guardian's mouth.

"A riddle," she realized, beaming with pleasure. "A place where North is South, eh?" She pressed her lips together, thinking, then snapped her fingers.

North Hall! It lay at the far *southern* edge of campus. That had to be what he meant. She didn't know what that bit about the "guardian's mouth" was all about, but there was one way to find out.

Bess jumped to her feet and raced toward the mall, heading south. "North Hall, here I come!"

CHAPTER 14

"**P**aul Cody, you are too much," Bess said to herself, fifteen minutes later.

She was standing in front of North Hall, an old brick building with a semicircular drive that led up to it from the mall. On either side of the stately doors was a bronze lion with its mouth open in a roar. One of the lions had a red helium balloon tied around its neck with a ribbon. Inside its open mouth was a package wrapped in tissue paper.

"Good job, guardian," Bess said, patting the lion's bronze mane and picking up the package. "You guarded whatever this is very well."

She ripped at the tissue paper, then hurriedly lifted the top off the box.

"Chocolates," she murmured. Two trays deep and five rows across. "Paul Cody, you will go to heaven for this."

Lying on top of the chocolates was a second envelope. "Another clue! I love it!" Bess cried.

She popped a chocolate into her mouth, then settled down to her second riddle:

> Come and share the balmy breeze
> Beneath the swaying, tall palm trees.

Palm trees? In Illinois? Bess had to think about that one for a while, but finally it came to her.

The greenhouse in the campus botanical garden. That had to be it. She'd never been there before, but she'd heard that it had different rooms to re-create the plant life of various geographical locations. There had to be palm trees in there somewhere.

The botanical garden was located just east, a few hundred yards from North Hall. The greenhouse turned out to be a sprawling complex of glassed-in domes and rooms. Bess had to make her way through the Living Desert and Asian Wetlands rooms before she finally came to an area that looked as though it belonged in a tropical rain forest—complete with a tiny waterfall, orchids, and other flowers in every color of the rainbow.

As Bess looked at the beautiful plants she saw something else that made her smile even more. "Paul!"

He was sitting on a bench underneath a palm tree draped with vines. His handsome features were filled with such tenderness that Bess felt her heart swell. "Hey, imagine running into you here," he said, shooting her a smile that lit up his whole face.

"As if you didn't know I was coming," she teased. She held out the box of chocolates as she sat down next to him. "Want one?"

Paul shook his head. "I'm holding out for something much sweeter," he said.

"Oh, yes?"

Bess felt her heart beating rapidly. Everything was so perfect. She breathed in the warm, humid air, listening to the gurgle of the waterfall. "I feel as if I'm on vacation somewhere far, far away," she said softly. "It's perfect."

"It *is* isolated. That was part of my plan," Paul admitted.

He turned and looked right into her eyes, and Bess felt her heart skip a beat. "What plan?" she asked, her voice barely a whisper.

"To have you all to myself. No auditions, no pledge pranks." He leaned slowly toward her, holding her with his mesmerizing gaze.

"No friends getting me upset," she said, slowly.

His face was just inches from hers now. He reached a hand around her waist, sending a delicious shiver through her. "Just you and me and this."

Then his lips closed over hers in a kiss that went on forever. When they finally pulled apart, Bess was tingling from head to toe.

"Wow," she whispered. "Definitely worth waiting for."

Paul brushed a finger against her cheek before leaning in again. "And this is just the beginning. . . ."

Nancy sighed, looking at the sea of students, faculty, and other visitors that filled the Kaplan Center for the Arts two weeks later, at the opening of the Wilder World of Art show. "Do you think we'll be able to actually see the artifacts?" she asked Jake, leaning close to him.

"Unlikely," he told her. "The thing about openings is that you tend to see a lot more people than art."

The seven artifacts that had been recovered from B. J. Olson were on display, along with fifteen other rare Cherokee pieces. After hearing that Will had the stolen items safely back in hand, Dan Chekelelee and the tribal officials had agreed to send up the rest of the artifacts right away.

"Will's show looks amazing!" Bess exclaimed as she and Paul squeezed through the crowd and joined Nancy and Jake.

"You're not going to get any argument from me," George added, walking up to the group of friends and grinning.

Nancy beamed back at her. "It really is a fantastic group of artifacts, George. Will should be so proud."

George laughed happily. "He is, believe me. Will said the college administration is even talking about doing a seminar on Cherokee art next semester. Maybe we can all go to it."

"Sure, that'd be great," Bess replied.

Paul nodded in agreement and added, "It looks like the World of Art series is getting off to a great start."

"Nancy!" A smiling Max Krauser materialized out the crowd next to them. "Nice to see you. That article you did on Helping Hands really helped us out. We've already got some volunteers for the Black and White Nights."

"Glad to hear it. By the way, I was serious about *my* offer to help out, too," she told him. She looked around, then grabbed Paul and Bess from a knot of people that included Holly Thornton, Eileen O'Connor, and a few of Nancy's suitemates. "Max Krauser, meet Paul Cody. He's the guy I was telling you about. And this is Bess Marvin."

"Whatever Nancy said about me, don't believe it," Paul said, holding his hands up defensively. "I'm a decent guy, I swear."

Max Krauser chuckled. "In that case, maybe you two wouldn't mind being part of the organizing committee for the Black and White Nights entertainment?"

"The Black and White Nights?" Bess echoed, her blue eyes sparkling with interest. "That's supposed to be the hottest event of the semester! Nancy, I bet you could get the Beat Poets to play."

"Sounds good to me," Max said with a grin.

"In fact, maybe all three of you could help out. It'd be a big help. Especially since I'm going to be away for a few weeks. My mother's been sick."

"Oh, I'm sorry," Nancy said.

Max gave her a warm smile. "She'll probably be okay, but I'd feel better about going home if I knew the entertainment was under control."

"I don't know," Paul said, shooting Bess a doubtful glance. "You and I working on a project together? Seeing each other for more than five or ten minutes at a stretch? Sounds kind of risky."

Nancy caught the confused expression on Bess's face. "What do you mean?" Bess asked.

"Well, I just mean that"—Paul caught her up and swung her around, so that Nancy, Jake, and Max had to jump back—"I might die of happiness!"

As her group of friends chatted, George looked around the gallery. She was bowled over by how beautiful it all looked—and apparently she wasn't the only one who felt that way. Ever since the opening had begun, the gallery had been swarming with visitors. George hadn't been able to get anywhere near Will, so many people were congratulating him and asking questions.

George's gaze flitted back and forth between her cousin Bess and Paul, taking in the special glances and smiles that flashed from one to the other. "Looks like you two are finally getting off to a good start," she murmured, crossing her arms over her chest. "It's about time."

Bess's cheeks turned pink with pleasure. "What can I say? I was waiting for the right guy to sweep me off my feet."

Bess started to drink her diet soda, then stopped and stared toward the gallery entrance. "Hey, there's Holly and Eileen," Bess said. "Let's go say hi."

Second later she and Paul were threading their way toward them. That's Bess, thought George. Running in a million different directions at once. George was about to follow, when Will stepped away from the people he was talking to and came over to her.

"It's definite!" he said. "The response to the show is already so good that the Anthropology Department is going to do a seminar on Native American cultures next semester."

"Fantastic!" George said, grinning up at him. He'd been so worried about letting down Dan Chekelelee and the other people of the Cherokee Nation. But now it looked as thought the exact opposite was happening.

"By the way, I like your new look," Will told her, looking down at the cane George was using instead of her crutches.

"The new me," she said. "The doctor says I won't even need this after another week or so."

"That's good, because you're going to have to be in good condition," Will told her.

He said it so mysteriously, George knew that something was up. "What for?"

Will's brown eyes sparkled with love as he bent to give her a huge hug. "For all the hiking and camping we'll do," he said into her ear, "when you and I go to visit the Cherokee Nation in Oklahoma one of these days . . . together."

"Do you see who I see?" Holly asked Bess, twenty minutes later.

Bess looked toward the gallery entrance, where Soozie Beckerman was standing in a pink silk cocktail dress that hugged all her curves. "The Ice Princess really went all out," Bess said in a low voice. "Looks like she even rented a date."

Soozie's hand rested on the arm of a tall guy with blond hair and classical good looks. "Kappa *is* the arty sorority," Holly put in. "I guess she felt that she should make a big impression."

Bess took a sip of her soda, then blinked as an idea came to her. "It would be a shame if anything happened to ruin the effect." She shot Holly a mischievous glance, holding up her cup. "Say, if something *spilled* on that fabulous dress she's wearing?"

"You are too devious," Holly said. "I love it!"

Bess followed Holly toward the entrance, where Soozie was smiling at everyone, as if she had just been crowned queen. "We never did get to talk to her about hiding that note and lying about us," Bess said.

"That's because she runs the other way whenever she sees us," Holly added. "But today we're not going to give her the chance. Sneak attack."

She plastered a huge smile on her face as she and Bess came up to Soozie and her date. "Soozie! Bess and I have been meaning to talk to you."

Soozie's smile froze on her face. "I don't see what we could possibly have to discuss." she said haughtily. But Bess noticed the uneasy flicker in her blue eyes.

"About the note I wrote to Holly?" Bess prompted. "The one you ripped up?"

"And the lies you told," Holly added. "Did you think we wouldn't find out?"

"I don't know what you're talking about," Soozie said. She shot an embarrassed glance at her date. "Anyway, this is hardly the time."

"You're right," Bess said, trying to sound apologetic. "We'll talk another time."

"Sorry to bother you," Holly added.

She gave Bess an imperceptible wink, then pretended to catch the toe of her shoe on the floor. "Whoops!"

Holly lurched forward, spilling her red wine down the front of Soozie's dress. Soozie jumped back with a gasp. When she saw the wide purple stain spreading down her front, her face went completely red.

"You idiot! Look what you've done!" she cried. "I can't go in there looking like this."

Bess couldn't bring herself to look at Holly. She knew she'd break up if she did.

Soozie stood there, looking back and forth from Bess to Holly. Then she grabbed her date's arm and said, "Come on. Let's get out of here."

As Soozie disappeared down the escalator, Bess raised up her hand, and Holly came through with a high five.

"Yes!" they crowed together.

Bess floated up the stairs to the second floor of Jamison Hall and headed down the hall toward her room. Paul's goodbye kiss still lingered on her lips, she was passing all of her classes, rehearsals would begin soon for the one-act plays, and she couldn't wait to start planning the entertainment for the Black & White Nights.

Could life possibly get any better than this? She seriously doubted it.

"Hi, Leslie," Bess said dreamily as she stepped into their room.

Leslie whirled around in her desk chair to glare at Bess. "Shut . . . up!" Leslie snapped, biting off the words.

Bess stopped cold. There were permanent rings beneath Leslie's eyes—Bess didn't think she'd slept more than a few hours in the past few days. Leslie's hair was a matted mess of knots, and her shirt wasn't even tucked in. Not only that, but her desk was buried under a disorganized clutter of books, papers, calculators, pencils, and diet soda bottles.

This wasn't the same Leslie King she'd been stuck with at the beginning of the year. It couldn't be. *That* Leslie King had creases ironed into all her pants and did a white-glove inspection at least three times a day.

"Leslie?" Bess asked worriedly. "Is there something I can do to—"

"How many times do I have to tell you!" Leslie burst out angrily. "If you can't stop yourself from making such a racket, then get out."

Bess bit her lip and sat silently down on her bed, staring at Leslie. She couldn't even bring herself to get mad at her roommate. She was too worried about her.

It looks as if Leslie's house of order is crashing down around her, thought Bess. What am I going to do?

Nancy held Jake's hand as he walked her back to Thayer Hall after the opening. "You were pretty quiet tonight when we were talking about the Black and White Nights," she said.

"I figured that was your territory. You're the one who wants to be a big sister." He turned her to face him, wrapping his arms around her waist. "I guess I was just speechless because we actually had some time together. I guess I'd rather spend it watching you than talking about casino gambling."

Jake's face glowed in the moonlight, and his eyes were filled with warmth. Standing there with him, she felt like the luckiest girl at Wilder.

"So," she said slowly, looking up at him.

"Does that mean you don't want to help out with Black and White Nights?"

"I'll do what I can." Jake smiled at her, but Nancy had the feeling that he was holding back.

"But?" she prompted.

He looked away for a moment, his eyes on the moon. "I've been spending more time over at the Animal Rescue League," he said. "I might not be able to put in as much work as you."

"Say no more." Nancy stood on tiptoe and kissed him on the lips. Jake's hands tightened around her, and the kiss went on and on.

"Wow," he whispered, when their mouths finally separated. "So I guess you're not angry."

"Not a bit," she said. "I figured I'd better get in some quality time while we have the chance. I have a feeling that from now on, you and I are the ones who are going to need to schedule ten-minute dates!"

Next in Nancy Drew on Campus™:

Ginny and Ray are majoring in romance, but they've got some major problems to deal with as well—like the little white lies Ginny's been telling her mom and dad, which could now come back to haunt her. Bess has a problem, too, but it's not about boyfriends. Her roommate, Leslie, has a shocking story to tell . . . about one of her professors. Nancy, meanwhile, is on the organizing committee for the gala Black & White Nights fund-raising event, and she's asked Jake to lend her a hand. But now they've got something else to collaborate on—for the *Wilder Times*. Leslie's story is spreading across campus, and it's getting more shocking by the minute: Her professor has turned up dead . . . in *Broken Promises*, Nancy Drew on Campus #9.

Christopher Pike presents . . .
a frighteningly fun new series for
your younger brothers and sisters!

SPOOKSVILLE™

The creepiest stories in town. . .

1 The Secret Path
53725-3/$3.50

2 The Howling Ghost
53726-1/$3.50

3 The Haunted Cave
53727-X/$3.50

4 Aliens in the Sky
53728-8/$3.99

5 The Cold People
55064-0/$3.99

6 The Witch's Revenge
55065-9/$3.99

7 Fright Night
52947-1/$3.99

By Christopher Pike

A MINSTREL® BOOK

Published by Pocket Books

Simon & Schuster Mail Order
200 Old Tappan Rd., Old Tappan, N.J. 07675

Please send me the books I have checked above. I am enclosing $_____ (please add $0.75 to cover the postage
and handling for each order. Please add appropriate sales tax). Send check or money order–no cash or C.O.D.'s
please. Allow up to six weeks for delivery. For purchase over $10.00 you may use VISA: card number, expiration
date and customer signature must be included.

Name _____

Address _____

City _____ State/Zip _____

VISA Card # _____ Exp.Date _____

Signature _____ 1175-03

Now your younger brothers or sisters can take a walk down Fear Street....

R·L·STINE'S

GHOSTS OF FEAR STREET®

1 Hide and Shriek
52941-2 / $3.99

2 Who's Been Sleeping in My Grave?
52942-0 / $3.99

3 Attack of the Aqua Apes
52943-9 / $3.99

4 Nightmare in 3-D
52944-7 / $3.99

5 Stay Away From the Treehouse
52945-5 / $3.99

6 Eye of the Fortuneteller
52946-3 / $3.99

7 Fright Knight
52947-1 / $3.99

A scary new series for the
younger reader from **R.L. Stine**

 A MINSTREL® BOOK

Published by Pocket Books

Simon & Schuster Mail Order
200 Old Tappan Rd., Old Tappan, N.J. 07675

Please send me the books I have checked above. I am enclosing $_____ (please add $0.75 to cover the postage and handling for each order. Please add appropriate sales tax). Send check or money order--no cash or C.O.D.'s please. Allow up to six weeks for delivery. For purchase over $10.00 you may use VISA: card number, expiration date and customer signature must be included.

Name _____

Address _____

City _____ State/Zip _____

VISA Card # _____ Exp.Date _____

Signature _____ 1180-03

NANCY DREW® AND THE HARDY BOYS®

TEAM UP FOR MORE MYSTERY...
MORE THRILLS...AND MORE
EXCITEMENT THAN EVER BEFORE!

A NANCY DREW AND HARDY BOYS SUPERMYSTERY™

☐	DOUBLE CROSSING	74616-2/$3.99
☐	A CRIME FOR CHRISTMAS	74617-0/$3.99
☐	SHOCK WAVES	74393-7/$3.99
☐	DANGEROUS GAMES	74108-X/$3.99
☐	THE LAST RESORT	67461-7/$3.99
☐	THE PARIS CONNECTION	74675-8/$3.99
☐	BURIED IN TIME	67463-3/$3.99
☐	MYSTERY TRAIN	67464-1/$3.99
☐	BEST OF ENEMIES	67465-X/$3.99
☐	HIGH SURVIVAL	67466-8/$3.99
☐	NEW YEAR'S EVIL	67467-6/$3.99
☐	TOUR OF DANGER	67468-4/$3.99
☐	SPIES AND LIES	73125-4/$3.99
☐	TROPIC OF FEAR	73126-2/$3.99
☐	COURTING DISASTER	78168-5/$3.99
☐	HITS AND MISSES	78169-3/$3.99
☐	EVIL IN AMSTERDAM	78173-1/$3.99
☐	DESPERATE MEASURES	78174-X/$3.99
☐	PASSPORT TO DANGER	78177-4/$3.99
☐	HOLLYWOOD HORROR	78181-2/$3.99
☐	COPPER CANYON CONSPIRACY	88514-6/$3.99
☐	DANGER DOWN UNDER	88460-3/$3.99
☐	DEAD ON ARRIVAL	88461-1/$3.99
☐	TARGET FOR TERROR	88462-X/$3.99
☐	SECRETS OF THE NILE	50290-5/$3.99
☐	A QUESTION OF GUILT	50293-x/$3.99

Simon & Schuster Mail Order
200 Old Tappan Rd., Old Tappan, N.J. 07675
Please send me the books I have checked above. I am enclosing $_____(please add $0.75 to cover the postage and handling for each order. Please add appropriate sales tax). Send check or money order--no cash or C.O.D.'s please. Allow up to six weeks for delivery. For purchase over $10.00 you may use VISA: card number, expiration date and customer signature must be included.

Name _____

Address _____

City _____ State/Zip _____

VISA Card # _____ Exp.Date _____

Signature _____

664-14

Boys. Clothes.
Popularity.
Whatever!

Cher is totally golden. She has *all* the answers...
so why shouldn't she run everybody's life?

A novel by H.B. Gilmour Based on the film written
and directed by Amy Heckerling
A major motion picture from Paramount

Zup with Cher?
Check out these books:

Cher Negotiates New York
A novel by Jennifer Baker

Can Cher and De rescue Tai from a random East Coast fate?

An American Betty in Paris
A novel by Randi Reisfeld

Josh in Paris? Cher in Beverly Hills? Not even! Cher
takes a way cultural trip. Can you say *boutique*?

Achieving Personal Perfection
A novel by H.B. Gilmour

Cher's buggin'—a major Baldwin wants to make *her* over.

1202